"Pretty weird," Glory replied. "Do you put all your women into training?"

One thick dark brow rose in inquiry. "Are you one of my women?"

Glory smiled. "Well, not yet, but that is the general idea, isn't it?"

His gaze swept over her body. "Most definitely," he said, his voice light. "I call it the dreaded-revenge scenario. The one where Randy Villain—boo, hiss— comes to collect on a dubious debt from our delicate but dedicated heroine, Miss Glory—oh, no, gasp, shudder. Twisting his handlebar mustache, our villain demands payment while his eyes are fixed on forbidden"—his gaze dropped to her bikini top—"but oh-so-tempting territory."

Glory picked up a handful of sand and, raising it above his head, released it slowly, watching it make a small pile on the top of his dark, disheveled hair.

There was silence for a moment. Then he spoke. "Glory, did you just pour sand on my head?"

Stealthily she began to scoot out of reach. "What?" she asked, sounding confused. "Oh, I know. It was probably a sand devil. You've heard of them? Sneaky little rascals, let me tell you. Kind of like the sandman, only they get you when you're trying to seduce innocent maidens." She looked at him, wide-eyed. "You run across them in Victorian novels a lot."

Alan nodded slowly, sand trickling down as he did. "Interesting."

Glory wasn't foolhardy; neither was she slow. Within seconds she was on her feet and running down the beach. But if she was quick, Alan was quicker. She hadn't made ten yards before he tackled her and exacted his revenge. . . .

WHAT ARE *LOVESWEPT* ROMANCES?

They are stories of true romance and touching emotion. We believe those two very important ingredients are constants in our highly sensual and very believable stories in the *LOVESWEPT* line. Our goal is to give you, the reader, stories of consistently high quality that may sometimes make you laugh, sometimes make you cry, but are always fresh and creative and contain many delightful surprises within their pages.

Most romance fans read an enormous number of books. Those they truly love, they keep. Others may be traded with friends and soon forgotten. We hope that each *LOVESWEPT* romance will be a treasure—a "keeper." We will always try to publish

LOVE STORIES YOU'LL NEVER FORGET
BY AUTHORS YOU'LL ALWAYS REMEMBER

The Editors

N N

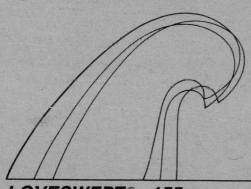

LOVESWEPT® • 155

Billie Green
Glory Bound

 BANTAM BOOKS
TORONTO • NEW YORK • LONDON • SYDNEY • AUCKLAND

GLORY BOUND

A Bantam Book / September 1986

Cover art by Steve Assel.

*If you would be interested in receiving protective vinyl
covers for your Loveswept books, please write to this address
for information:*

Loveswept
Bantam Books
P.O. Box 985
Hicksville, NY 11802

ISBN 0-553-21769-0

Published simultaneously in the United States and Canada

*Bantam Books are published by Bantam Books, Inc. Its
trademark, consisting of the words "Bantam Books" and
the portrayal of a rooster, is Registered in U.S. Patent
and Trademark Office and in other countries. Marca
Registrada. Bantam Books, Inc., 666 Fifth Avenue, New York,
New York 10103.*

PRINTED IN THE UNITED STATES OF AMERICA

O   0 9 8 7 6 5 4 3 2 1

One

"A blind date." Alan Spencer shook his head in disbelief: he was spending the evening with an unknown woman. He muttered again, "And it amounts to nothing more than an asinine, sophomoric, pain-in-the-butt blind date."

As he pulled his rented Lincoln to a stop in the wide, curving driveway, he stared at the massive front door of the Wainwright house. Built on three levels, the sprawling structure had clean, modern lines, and in no way merited the frown with which he viewed it. Although he lived in Dallas, Alan was quite familiar with this exclusive Austin enclave, where a prospective resident had to be voted in, and security fences, gates, and guards came with membership in the community. This expensive property, this secure way of life, were purchased with the fortunes made from cattle, oil, airlines, and other ventures.

For a moment Alan simply sat where he was, suppressing the almost overpowering urge to drive away. Social functions were a part of his life that he accepted with equanimity, but this civilized equivalent of an ancient mating ritual brought out in him an equally ancient instinct for survival.

Flexing his shoulders in resignation, he opened the car door. There were reasons for his being here tonight, he told himself firmly as he stepped onto the pavement. If he could get to know George Wainwright on a more personal level, the man himself outside the conference room, surely they could come to some kind of agreement on the Svensen project.

The Svensen project was Alan's baby. He had fought his own board of directors for it a year ago. And for six months he had worked his ass off to get negotiations under way. All other detailed aspects of the project had fallen together beautifully. Now it only remained for Wainwright to lend his company's cooperation to the effort. If everything went as planned, within two years Spencer-Houghton International and Wainwright, Inc., could have a vital segment of the electronics market wrapped up.

But Wainwright, a man with a reputation for being stubborn, was resisting. It wasn't as though Alan were proposing a merger. He merely wanted the cooperation of Wainwright, whose company held a key patent. The deal would be beneficial to both organizations. But the older man was suspicious of working with Alan's people, and he didn't hesitate to show it. Alan had to break the deadlock one way or another.

As he approached the front door, he felt his shoulder muscles tense again. He hadn't gotten to the age of thirty-seven without running across a few dedicated matchmakers, proud fathers or uncles or brothers who would like nothing better than to have a Spencer of Spencer-Houghton International in the family. Using native cunning, he had managed to avoid their machinations.

But this time Alan had agreed willingly. After all, he had assured himself, what did it matter if Wainwright's darling debutante daughter had acne or picked her teeth with a matchbook cover? The important thing was that he and Wainwright gain some kind of rapport with each other. He firmly believed they could do that in an informal setting, away from the underlying pressures of a business environment. The presence of Wainwright's daughter—damn! He had forgotten her name—was an unavoidable annoyance.

By the time the maid who had opened the door for him had escorted him across the stark white entry hall, Alan was once again resigned to the necessity of this occasion. Walking into the large, paneled study, he settled a practiced social smile on his somewhat austere face. He was ready to be bored in a good cause.

George Wainwright was standing with his back to Alan, pouring a glass of wine. He was a stout man with thinning hair who managed to convey an air of good-breeding at all times and even the appearance of elegance every once in a while.

Standing at double French doors was a woman Alan presumed was his blind date; her back was also turned to him and the room at large. Since she stood in the shadows, the only thing he could be positive of was that she was small.

At the sound of his footsteps, both people in the room turned toward Alan simultaneously. Wainwright smiled in enthusiastic welcome, but it was the woman who made Alan's eyes widen and his pulse quicken. All at once he felt short of breath, as though someone had thrown an unexpected punch to his solar plexus, because the "unavoidable annoyance" was breathtakingly lovely. The whole was so sensational, it took a moment for him to assimilate the separate features that combined to make that whole. Her lustrous black hair was pulled back from a center part and rolled in a V at the base of her small head. Her facial features were finely chiseled, suggesting fragility and innocence and the freshness of youth. The off-the-shoulder blue dress she wore allowed the view of an exceptional amount of flesh that seemed the color and texture of a camellia, and made a startling contrast to her raven hair. When she smiled—merely a small, wistful curving of gentle red lips—it was as though a cameo had come to life.

Suddenly Alan realized his host was speaking to him, and he brought himself back to reality with a jerk, hoping his lapse hadn't been noticed.

"—so glad you could come, Spencer," Wainwright was saying. "I like for my little Glory to meet my business associates." He laughed heartily. "After all, business pays for the goodies. Besides, she needs to know what's happening."

Alan smiled weakly and nodded. He still felt disoriented, almost as though he were hung over, from the shock of seeing Wainwright's daughter. To say she was not what he had expected was a massive understatement.

"Come meet Gloria," the older man said. "Glory, this is Alan Spencer."

The vision walked—no, floated—forward, her small, slender hand extended. The delicacy of her features amazed him. He had seen exquisite bisque china that would look gross compared to her skin texture and color. And her eyes—he had never seen eyes so blue. All the colors that went into her makeup were vivid and true. Blue and cream and red and black. The light touched her black hair and was trapped, seeming to come from within the shining stuff. Her name was perfect because she was glorious.

"How do you do?" she said, her voice soft and musical.

Alan made the necessary response, hoping his state of mind was not obvious. He prided himself on always being in control, but holding her hand took his mind away from everything but her. As she stood beside him, he noticed again what a small woman she was, making him, at six feet, feel taller than he ever had before.

"Sit down, Alan, and name your poison," Wainwright said.

When he managed to tear his gaze away from

Gloria, he realized he was still holding her hand
Dropping it regretfully, he said, "I'll have scotch
and water, please."

This was ridiculous, he thought wryly. He knew
why he was here, and it had nothing to do with the
lovely Gloria. Turning toward his host, he said
almost in desperation, "I see Parker came up with
that report after all."

Any answer Wainwright might have made was
lost on Alan when Glory moved to the chair opposite him and lowered herself gracefully into it.

He wondered if she was used to people staring at
her. He hoped so, because he couldn't seem to take
his eyes off her. Accepting a drink from his host
he said, "Your father tells me you live in Dallas
Gloria."

"Call her Glory," Wainwright said good
naturedly. "Everyone does. Yes, Glory has her own
place in Dallas." Wainwright glanced away, but not
before Alan saw his lips tighten. "For almost five
years she's lived there. I can't abide the city myself
I wouldn't set foot there if they gave me the place."

Gloria stared silently at her hands, but Alan
could feel a tension in the room that hadn't been
present before. Dallas was evidently a point of
dispute between father and daughter.

Before the silence in the room became uncomfortable, Wainwright smiled. "I miss Glory, but
women nowadays have to spread their wings, eh
Alan? As soon as she gets enough of the fast pace
and fast people in Dallas, she'll come back to her
hometown." He glanced indulgently at his daugh-

ter. "You should hear her talk about all the parties she goes to. I call her my beautiful sybarite."

Glory didn't comment, but she smiled . . . and Alan was dazzled. He continued to be dazzled all through the elaborate dinner. He hoped he wouldn't be quizzed on the menu, because he had no idea what he ate. Glory rarely spoke, but when she did, her words were soft, like a melody from gentler times. After a while Alan decided she was shy. She never initiated a topic of conversation and rarely contributed to one introduced by the two men. But there was a serenity about her that was, in its way, as intriguing as if she'd been a lively conversationalist. She seemed in some way removed from the ordinary world, her constant smile reflecting the beauty of her thoughts.

Occasionally Alan would remember his reason for coming to dinner and would make an effort to get to know his host. The atmosphere he had wished for was present. They had numerous interests in common, and the relaxing environment allowed them to be a little more open than at their usual business meeting. Personalities began to mesh rather that clash.

As they rose from the table, Alan felt he had accomplished his purpose. The dinner had gone smoothly, and he was reasonably satisfied that a rapport had been established that would help at their next business meeting.

They were laughing when they walked again into the study. In a carefully casual movement, Wainwright glanced at his watch. "I'm afraid I'm going to have to leave you now, Alan. I'm expecting a call at ten." He laughed. "Too bad there aren't international business hours. After I take care of this business, I think I'll call it a night. I tend to hit the sack earlier these days."

Alan nodded, unalarmed at the obvious ploy to leave him alone with Glory. Because with as much intensity as Alan had dreaded it earlier, he now welcomed the moment that he would be free to give all his attention to the lovely woman standing silently beside him.

As soon as the door closed behind his host, Alan followed her to the couch, sitting beside her. He stared down into the depths of her clear blue eyes. He felt compelled to unravel the mystery he saw there. What was she thinking? What was she feeling? Did she know that he was totally captivated by her?

"This is a wonderful room," he said, his eyes holding amusement as he studied her face. "Too bad your father couldn't afford all new furniture."

She stared blankly at him for a moment, then glanced around the room at the Louis XIV furniture, which was mixed to esthetic perfection with modern pieces. "These are antiques." she said. "Daddy paid a lot of money for them."

"That was a joke," he said ruefully. "A bad one, I'll admit, but still a joke."

"Oh. Yes, of course, a joke," she said, then smiled hesitantly.

He watched her silently for a moment, then his lips twisted in a self-mocking smile. "I have to be honest with you," he said quietly, unable to take his gaze from her face. "I really didn't want to come here tonight."

"Oh?" she said. Then, bringing a dainty lace handkerchief to her lips, she lay a slim hand on her perfect breasts and belched delicately.

"It was the duck," she explained, the softness of her voice making it sound almost monotone. "It always lays on my chest." She smiled. "Now, what were you saying, Alan?"

Alan glanced away from her, feeling more than a little confused. He swallowed heavily and said, "I forgot." Although he tried to recapture his original thought, it had escaped him. Drawing in a slow breath, he said, "Do you like living in Dallas?"

"Yes," she said, then smiled, and the silence fell around them again.

"It's strange that we haven't met there," he said. "I attend a lot of social functions."

"Yes, strange," she murmured.

Something was definitely wrong here, Alan thought, deep grooves appearing between his eyes as the silence drew out again. "I'm sorry your father doesn't approve of Dallas," he said at last. "It must make living there difficult for you."

"Yes."

Rubbing a hand along his jaw, experiencing extreme mental discomfort, he shifted positions. "I like it myself. There's always plenty to do . . . always something new happening . . . always . . ." His voice faded away at the end of the sentence, making the thought seem as lethargic as the atmosphere in the room. He cleared his throat noisily. "I understand he sends his plane for you quite frequently."

"Yes, he does."

"That's good." The scar on his cheek twitched uncontrollably. "At least . . . at least you get to see each other often."

"Yes."

Alan was beginning to panic. It was difficult to understand how a dream had turned so swiftly into a nightmare. Talking to her was like wading through molasses. "What do you do in Dallas?" he asked.

"Do?" she asked, her expression slightly confused.

"Yes, your work. What do you do?"

"Work?" She smiled serenely. "Oh, I don't work. My constitution is too delicate."

"That's too bad," he said, his voice vague. He stood, and shoving his hands into the pockets of his slacks, walked to the French doors. He glanced out at the moonlit garden in desperation. "The moon is beautiful tonight, almost full. A perfect night for a drive," he said inanely, feeling like a babbling ass.

"I get carsick," she said, smiling.

To Alan the smile was beginning to look slightly imbecilic. He murmured something he hoped sounded suitably sympathetic, then opened the door a few inches. "We could go for a walk in the garden."

"The night air affects my chest," she said sweetly.

"It probably likes lying around with the duck," he muttered under his breath.

When he turned away from the double doors, her slim shoulders were shaking slightly, then she sneezed violently and smiled. "I'm sorry, Alan," she said sweetly. "What were you saying?"

"Nothing. Nothing at all." He drew in a breath to begin again. "Since you don't work, you must have time to indulge in hobbies," he said hopefully.

When she smiled, he gritted his teeth.

"Hobbies are for people who need a diversion from an otherwise unfulfilling life. My father is very wealthy." She shrugged daintily. "I don't need hobbies." Then again she fell silent.

"Leisure is nice," he said awkwardly. "I always seem to be rushing from one meeting to another. And when I'm not working, I try to cram a maximum of activity into a minimum of time. I buy all the latest best sellers, then have to read them bits at a time before I go to bed. It must be nice to have the time to sit down and read one straight through."

This time her smile touched a nerve, and Alan flinched visibly.

"I have an astigmatism that prohibits extensive reading," she said, and at this point Alan wouldn't have been surprised to see her beautiful eyes cross, "but I keep abreast of current works by having my maid read the reviews to me . . . *New York Times*, of course."

"Of course," he echoed. Somehow, he should have known. She didn't work or read and had no hobbies. He wondered if she had her maid attend parties for her as well, carefully editing the gossip for the interesting bits.

In exasperation he said, "Do you ever *think* about anything interesting?"

Her beautiful eyes widened and for a moment Alan could have sworn he saw laughter in them, but when she began to cough into her handkerchief, he knew it had been wishful thinking on his part.

"Alan," she gasped. "It's the damp night air. Could you please close the door?"

"Of course." He closed the door behind him, making a genuine effort not to slam it in frustration. He had had enough. All evening he had imagined gentle, intelligent, even fascinating thoughts flowing through her mind, merely to find the only thing flowing there was a gentle breeze.

His lips twitched irresistibly. Exasperation had given way at last to humor, which made the situation potentially dangerous. If he stayed any longer, he was in danger of embarrassing everyone concerned either by falling asleep or bursting out in hysterical laughter.

"Miss—Gloria," he said, his voice kind but resolute. "It's been a delightful evening, but I'm afraid all the excitement has worn me out. I'd better be going." He moved slowly toward the door and escape. "Tell your father I'll be in touch."

She stood and smiled. "Yes, of course." She extended her hand. "Since we both live in Dallas, my father expects us to see each other again. Be sure to call at least two weeks in advance so I can fit you in."

"Yes, yes," he stuttered, barely touching her hand as he began to move backward. "I'll do that."

"Actually," she said, her voice smooth and colorless. "I'm flying back to Dallas tonight in Daddy's plane. Why don't we share the ride?"

"That would be . . . wonderful, but I'm afraid I still have some business to catch up on." He smiled, shrugging. "You've lived with your father long enough to know how business is. Maybe another time."

He ducked through the door, and seconds later he was in his car, his foot pressing the accelerator to the floor. The night had turned out exactly as he had wanted it to. He and Wainwright had established a better relationship. He had learned about George Wainwright, the man behind the business. That was good, he assured himself.

Suddenly he burst out laughing, the sound filling the empty interior of the Lincoln. Alan had learned something about himself tonight too. He had learned that he, Alan Spencer, at his age and experience, had for one short period of time believed in fairy tales.

Two

Houston, Texas

"The problem is, Alan, my stockbroker didn't know a thing about the merger, so I missed out completely. Peterson's man knew all about it, and he's cleaning up. So what do you think, should I change?"

Making a carefully noncommittal reply, Alan grabbed a glass of champagne from a tray carried by a passing waiter. Taking a sip, he glanced around the huge ballroom. Scattered about the edges of the room were trees, representing autumn he supposed, but the trees and the leaves were covered with gold foil, representing, rather, the people in the room. Or so he supposed. Alan's lips twisted in a wry smile. You just couldn't convince some people that Midas was not a happy man.

The scene, on the surface, looked like a crowd of beautiful people mingling socially. Hundreds of the "best" people were gathered, ostensibly for charity, in reality for the glory of Tess Wollencott, noted Houston socialite. Each guest appeared to be enjoying the companionship of friends from across the country, but if an observer looked more closely, if he moved through the room eavesdropping, he would learn that this was simply an extension of a business lunch. People were wheeling and dealing in every part of the room, building empires and tearing them down again. They were playing the power game at the buffet table—pick up a couple of million in front of the pâté, double it at the lobster mousse, then lose it all at the créme brûlée.

The scene was not unique or even new, but tonight Alan was a little tired of it all. Tonight he felt the disquieting urge for a conversation that had to do with nothing more urgent than the weather.

He almost laughed aloud, thinking of the conversation to end all conversations. That night with Glory Wainwright should have cured him of his need for nonbusiness discussions. On the surface it had been an extremely forgettable night. But strangely, her face had remained an irritating, unwelcome memory that he couldn't seem to shake.

In the three weeks since he had had dinner with George Wainwright, Alan and the older man had met twice in Austin. Alan had been a little wary at their first meeting, hoping he had not blown the deal by ducking out on that delicate flower, Wainwright's daughter. But to his surprise, Wainwright had been extremely gracious.

Although the older man's attitude was puzzling personally, Alan wasn't about to question him. Things were going too smoothly. Negotiations were progressing slowly, but at long last they were progressing. The Svensen project was finally on the horizon of possibility.

Hearing Wainwright's name, Alan turned his attention back to the group of men around him.

". . . and Wainwright won't say a thing," one of the men was saying. "Come on, Alan, give. What's going on between you and the Austin wonder?"

Alan smiled stiffly. "Don't panic, Phil. There's not going to be a merger." He glanced around the room. "When did you talk to Wainwright? Is he here?"

"No, I talked to him last week. He left two days ago for a month's vacation in Mexico." The man smiled broadly. "But I for one don't miss him, not with the substitute he sent."

The talk drifted again into stock market gossip as Alan wondered which of Wainwright's men had been sent in his place. Probably Brody or McDaniels, neither of whom would do Alan any good if he were in the mood to talk business, which he definitely was not.

The urgency that always seemed to be in the air when powerful men gathered was stifling tonight, pushing Alan toward the doors that stood open to the mansion's grounds.

Outside, the terraced garden was softly lit by strategically placed spotlights. Alan walked slowly, a nagging discontent picking and poking at his mind. He frowned. Maybe he was dissatisfied because the Svensen project no longer needed his constant attention. It had taken so much of his time and energy in the last year that the resolution of the problems concerning it left a hole in Alan's life. He was in a state of limbo, unable to start a new project until the details of this one were taken care of.

Turning a corner, he saw a group of people a few yards away . . . and at the center was Glory Wainwright. His heart jumped crazily, the sight of her loveliness affecting him against his will.

Tonight she wore a shimmering silver floor-length dress that clung to her figure like a sheet of moonlit water. Her shining ebony hair was pulled up and back in a Psyche knot, completing the ethereal picture of untouchable beauty.

Alan took an instinctive step toward her, then reality returned and he shook his head roughly, like a dog emerging from an unexpected dip in the lake.

Hell, he thought. Gloria Wainwright was the last person he wanted to run into. He had come through the last encounter with his professional relationship with her father intact. The next time he might not be so lucky. He clenched his fingers, knowing he would have felt a lot more comfortable if she had grown ugly in the time since he had last seen her.

When he realized the group was walking slowly toward him, Alan ducked behind an incredibly ugly statue, feeling slightly ridiculous but justified. They paused a few feet away, and although he tried to ignore them, Alan was forced into the role of eavesdropper as he leaned against the smooth carved marble.

"Come on, Gloria," a man said. "Tell Sami about the time you walked in on Harvey Samuelson and the Van Meters' Swedish au pair."

"I've always suspected you were a gossip, Chip," Glory said, her voice dry, "but I never knew you were a long-distance voyeur. Why do you want me to keep telling that story? Is this some kind of time-share titillation?"

"Tell me, Glory," a girl said coaxingly. "We've all been chased around the room by Harvey; he deserves the gossip. Chippie said his toupee was slipping down on his nose when you walked in on them."

"If I remember right, Harvey's hair was resting in a much more embarrassing place," Glory said, her voice filled with laughter, "but I'm not going to repeat the story. I would never have told Chip if he hadn't been standing in the hall when I came out of the bedroom."

As they talked, Alan slowly straightened away from the statue, a confused frown worrying his lips. Something here wasn't right. This wasn't the Glory he remembered. Her voice was too alive, too vibrant.

"Glory was doubled over laughing," the man called Chip said. "I wanted to peek, but she wouldn't let me."

"It was for your own good," Glory said. "One look

at the magnificance of those Swedish thighs and you would have been a goner."

"She was a little hefty, wasn't she?" another man said. "I always wondered why the Van Meters shipped her back to Sweden so fast. Magnificent thighs, you say?"

"That's enough," Glory said, chuckling. "Can't we talk about something wholesome . . . or at least clothed? Has anyone been to New York lately? What are the clothes like for fall? I haven't been to a fashion show in eons."

For Alan, listening to her speaking casually to her friends brought revelation. There was animation and contagious humor in her voice. The earlier confusion left him, his eyes narrowing as it was replaced by a growing conviction that the lovely Glory was a master at playing games . . . and he had been the dumb shmuck who had fallen hook, line, and sinker for one of them.

He had to force himself to remain still when he heard her laugh. The sound floated through the garden like musical notes. Anger that had been building dissolved immediately. He still wanted to get his hands on her beautiful throat, but not to strangle her.

When he heard her laugh again, his curiosity grew too strong to resist. Alan moved in the shadows until he could see the group. Glory was dancing with a blond young man. In his arms she whirled around, her head thrown back, the silver fabric of her gown floating out to expose tantalizing glimpses of shapely calves and silver-shod feet. She looked so lively, so wonderfully vital. So much the enchanting fraud.

Alan leaned back against the statue, biding his time. A few minutes later, as though he had planned it, the group with her moved on, leaving Glory behind. He walked slowly from behind the statue.

She didn't see him at once as she stood staring up at the star-filled sky. Drenched in moonlight, her silver gown an unearthly part of it, she seemed a moon maiden on a brief visit to Earth.

When gravel shifted beneath his feet, she turned to glance at him. They stood silently, staring at each other, and he saw instant recognition in her face and another emotion he couldn't identify.

After a moment she closed her eyes, as though willing him to go away. Then a second later she opened her eyes and said slowly, "Oh, my . . . Mr. Spencer."

"Yes, and as difficult as it is to believe," Alan said, his dark eyes sparkling, "you are Miss Wainwright of the permanent mental ennui."

He examined the face before him silently, reading the chagrin in her incredible blue eyes. Several times since the dinner with Wainwright, Alan had dreamed of her face, *this* face, not the vapid caricature he had seen that night. Now there was no vacant stare, no simple-minded smile. This face was alive, filled with spirit and intelligence.

An irresistible smile twitched at his strong lips. "This is a very interesting development, don't you think?"

She shifted in visible discomfort. "Mr. Spencer—"

"Alan," he corrected her, still studying her face. "Why did you want me to think you were a beautiful eggplant?"

"It's very complicated," she said, her voice wary, her eyes alert.

Leaning against the statue, he crossed his arms. "For you, I might be able to make time," he said, smiling. "I have to admit the whole thing smacks of a plot too intricate for my humble mind."

Glancing down, she played with a bit of silver fabric draped at her hip. She avoided his eyes, obviously unwilling to explain herself.

"Maybe if I recap this thing, you can show me where I lost it." He rubbed his jaw thoughtfully. "Three weeks ago I allowed a business associate, one George Wainwright, to talk me into spending an evening with his daughter. I figured said daughter would be a real dog . . . otherwise why would her father have to find dates for her? Imagine my surprise"—his gaze traced the lines of her face—"when the 'dog' turned out to be the loveliest woman I had ever set eyes on."

She stared somewhere beyond his left shoulder. "This is not necessary," she said, her voice slightly husky and incredibly sexy.

"Oh, I think it is. Yes, I think it's absolutely necessary," he murmured before continuing. "During the course of the evening, as I watched this vision, I began to be more and more captivated by her. It wasn't just her loveliness that drew me; there was something deep in her eyes, something that seemed to reach out to me."

As he spoke, he caught and held her gaze, searching for some spark of memory, for even a minute recurrence of that first moment of attraction. But Glory had evidently decided to shut him out. There was no decipherable expression in her clear blue eyes.

Shrugging slightly, he rocked back on his heels, thrusting his hands into his pants pockets. "When it turned out that the beautiful lady had no animation," he continued, "not a single thought in her lovely head, I felt as though I had just been told there was no tooth fairy. Now it seems that the lady was not what she pretended to be. She had deliberately led me to believe that she was an orchid . . . for purposes we have yet to discover."

She smiled, a small, wry movement of soft lips. "I suppose you have a right to be angry at the way I deceived you."

"Do I sound angry?"

Glancing up, she studied his features. "No, you don't. You sound . . . relieved," she said, her expression puzzled.

Sharp lady, Alan thought. He *was* relieved. The dreams had been too strong. He didn't like the idea of being obsessed with the empty-headed thing he had imagined her to be. But this woman, this lovely, intelligent woman, was worthy of an obsession.

She stared at him for a moment and her lips parted to speak, then in the distance they heard laughter, and she blinked.

"I've really got to get back inside," she said, moving slowly toward the house. "I'm supposed to be circulating."

He grasped her slender arm, intending to demand an explanation. But as he felt the smooth flesh beneath his hand, the words evaporated in his throat. Staring down at his dark fingers pressed against her white skin, he felt dumbstruck. He couldn't even remember what he had intended to say. His mouth was unexplainably dry, his breathing shallow.

As though the touch also affected her, Glory became very still. Slowly she raised her eyes to his.

"Lovely," he whispered huskily as he stared down at her face. "When I remembered how your father talked about you as though you were the original party animal, I thought he must be blind . . . or nuts." He moved closer, watching her breasts rise and fall swiftly. "But now, without the charade, I see that this"—he waved a hand toward the ballroom—"is your element. You were made to sparkle, inside and out."

When he leaned his head toward her, she made no effort to stop him. It was as though she were caught up in the same spell. It seemed natural when they moved into each other's arms. Slowly he lowered his head until his lips touched hers, closing his eyes to let the feeling wash over him. Incredibly his hand was shaking when it moved down her back, tentatively testing her bare back and the soft silver-gilt-covered curves.

When the kiss ended, she leaned her head against him. He kissed the soft vulnerable spot below her ear, then the hollow of her throat, enchanted to hear her draw in a sharp breath.

She reached up to gently touch his face. "Alan," she said, her voice low and husky. "I'm representing Daddy tonight. I have to go back."

He knew it was the truth, but resisted for a moment because he didn't want to let her go. They were virtual strangers, yet he felt as though they had just rolled out of bed after a long night of lovemaking.

Inhaling slowly, he said, "You're right. We can talk later." The look he gave her was determined. "There are a few questions I need answers to. But in the meantime there's no reason I can't stand beside you while you represent your father, is there?"

She glanced away for a second, then looked back at him and smiled. "No reason," she agreed softly. Then, as they started moving toward the house, she turned toward him. "I'm afraid my lipstick is gone." Her laugh was light, almost breathless. "I'd better make a trip to the powder room or the gossips will have a field day."

Her gaze barely grazed his face as she reached up to touch his lapel, then let her hand fall. "I'll meet you by the buffet in five minutes."

Alan didn't want to take his hand from around her waist, but he did at the last minute, just before they walked back into the ballroom. He watched her walk across the room and smiled, his senses dazzled. He was going to enjoy unraveling the mysteries of Glory.

He had no patience for the chitchat that went on

around him as he stood waiting, and spoke only when directly addressed. It was forty-five minutes before Alan finally decided he was the world's biggest sucker . . . because Glory obviously wasn't coming back.

Three

Dallas, Texas

"We'll have to park here. The parking lot that goes with the building is locked."

Alan nodded and pulled the Mercedes over to the curb. Leaving the car behind, Alan and Fred Zeigler, real estate broker, began to walk down the sidewalk.

Alan glanced around the area with interest. He was unfamiliar with this part of the city. He usually merely drove through it on his way to somewhere else. But if he were going to become a part of this community, even through his business, he wanted to know it.

The buildings were old and without personality. And although this area was close to downtown Dallas, the people on the streets could have lived in another world. Downtown there were women and men of all races, dressed for success, with purpose

26

to their steps, their carriage exuding barely subdued confidence.

In this older part of Dallas there was also a mixture of races, but there the similarity to downtown ended. The people on the streets here were similar to each other in the same way the successful people were similar to each other, not in outward appearance only, but in the way they all walked, slowly, with no important meetings to get to, nothing pressing waiting at the end of the street. And if their carriage exuded anything, it was wariness of their fellow man.

Alan was one of several Dallas businessmen who were investigating the feasibility of revitalizing this older part of Dallas by transferring some of their divisions here. The project was new, merely in the discussion stage, but Alan wanted to see the physical setting before he proceeded. He wanted to be able to discuss the pros and cons with something more than facts on paper to draw from.

Zeigler, in his carefully tailored three-piece suit, looked distinctly uncomfortable in this part of town, and as they walked, began to look as wary as the people they passed.

Alan couldn't have endured wearing a suit on Saturday. The first day of the weekend was his day at the gym, even when he had business to take care of. As he had today, he usually showed up in a sweat suit and Adidases.

They passed a vacant weed-covered lot, and although Fred didn't even glance at the kids playing there, Alan took it all in with sharp eyes.

Rubbish covered most of the lot, but in the center was a rough baseball diamond and lots of kids. Except for two teenagers, the majority appeared to be twelve or younger, all taking advantage of a fine Saturday afternoon.

"This is it," the real estate man said, his voice sounding overly hearty as he stopped at the brick building adjacent to the vacant lot.

The lock on the front door looked permanent and took several minutes to maneuver. Inside, dust and dirt was everywhere. The two men walked through the empty building, pausing occasionally so that Zeigler could look through his papers to explain a particular feature.

Although the building seemed to be structurally sound, it was a dreary place. If Alan bought it, the first order would be to brighten the place up. People became alcoholics in this kind of dreariness.

On the third floor they stopped to look at possible office space. Zeigler gingerly opened a window to allow air into the stuffy room. The sounds of the kids playing drifted up to them, and Alan walked to the window.

As he stared down at them, a reminiscent smile grew on his face. Rough and ready baseball must bring memories to a lot of people, he thought as he watched them play.

"That lot would make a good place for executive parking," Zeigler said. "It wouldn't take much to clear it."

"No," Alan said.

At the apparent confirmation of his opinion, the man grew expansive. "A couple of 'dozers—"

"I mean, no, it wouldn't make a good parking lot," Alan said, his voice quiet but firm. "If I buy the building, the baseball diamond stays."

The man looked at him as if he were crazy, but merely said, "If that's what you want."

It was an answer Alan was used to, and he didn't give the man any notice. He was more interested in the kids below. As he watched, the sun caught the black ponytail of one of the teenagers, who was now standing on third base. Her hair sparkling with multicolored light, the girl leaned forward, her hand on one knee as though prepared to steal home.

Alan smiled. She had probably joined the game to keep an eye on her kid brother. He had done the same thing often enough in his younger years, back when his brother had been a Little Leaguer.

The girl's hair reminded him of Glory's. He frowned suddenly, annoyed that he couldn't stop thinking about her. He wanted to see her again, and not only to find out what was going on with her. He needed to find out what was going on with himself. She affected him too strongly for comfort.

But he had found that Glory wasn't listed in the telephone book, and he couldn't very well call George Wainwright on his vacation demanding his daughter's address. He would simply have to wait until the man returned from Mexico.

"Knock me home, Billy! Come on, you can do it!"

Immediately Alan stiffened, standing straighter as he heard the shout of the teenager below. Only it wasn't a teenage girl, and she definitely wasn't playing ball with her kid brother.

Swiveling sharply, Alan left the real estate man in the room without explanation and took the stairs down, two at a time. Outside the building, he stepped over a pile of discarded tires and walked across the vacant lot toward the diamond.

Glory was sliding into home plate when he reached her. Bending down, he grasped her arm to pull her to her feet. She stood up, laughing, then turned to him, and the laughter died instantly.

"Oh . . . wow," she whispered, clearly stunned by his presence.

Still holding her arm, Alan walked away from the kids, forcing her to walk with him. When they reached the shadow of the wall, he turned toward her. His gaze ran over her. No artful makeup covered her face, only a few smudges. Black curls tumbled untidily around her cheeks. She wore a gray sweatshirt and tight, faded jeans hugged her hips.

"Now, what in hell is going on?" Alan asked, feeling confused and annoyed and wonderfully exhilarated all at the same time.

As he spoke, he pulled a handkerchief from his breast pocket and began to wipe the dirt from her face. "Who are you? The brain-dead Miss Wainwright? Gloria, the social butterfly? Or Andy Hardy's sister?" He scrubbed at a spot, ignoring her wince. "What are you doing here?"

"Playing baseball."

"Don't give me that. You ducked out on me in Houston—stick out your tongue." He dampened the handkerchief, then applied it to her chin. "I felt like a fool. The time in Austin wasn't enough. You had to do it to me again. But Houston was the last time. Do you hear? This time I'm going to get answers."

She tilted her head, staring up at him silently. His hand stilled and he felt as though someone had stuck a cattle prod to him.

"You've got freckles," he said huskily, feeling that he had made an important discovery.

"Not many," she whispered, her sapphire eyes never leaving his.

"Six—no seven." He reached up to run a finger over the bridge of her nose. Then slowly he leaned down to kiss one freckle that had escaped the crowd and dwelt just below her left eye. He was drawn irresistibly into the blue sensuality of her eyes.

Oh, no, not again, he thought fleetingly before he lowered his mouth to hers. Then all thought fled as his lips covered hers.

She made a small almost undetectable movement into him, her breasts pressing into his chest. Groaning, he wrapped his hands around her waist, pulling her closer.

"Mr. Spencer!"

Releasing Glory reluctantly, Alan turned and saw Zeigler. The man was breathing hard as he headed toward them, and Alan decided quickly to meet him halfway. He'd get rid of Zeigler fast and get down to serious business. . . . Gloria. He preemptorily dismissed the man, then impatiently turned back to Glory. "Now—"

She was gone.

Swinging around, Alan kicked a beer bottle in frustration. Dammit, he would find her if he had to tear down the whole town. And next time he wouldn't get closer than three feet. She was dangerous. The only way he was going to get answers was to keep her well within sight every second . . . and out of his arms.

Four

It was well after midnight when Glory pulled her bright red Corvette onto the well-lit street where she had lived for four years. The street was dotted with renovated early-twentieth-century houses.

Trying to recapture the glamour of another era was the "in" thing of the moment for wealthy young Dallas couples, and this particular street had been a real find for the renovation-minded. Several of the houses had been featured in *House Beautiful*, and deservedly so.

A couple of blocks down the street Glory turned into the gravel drive of a worn three-story house. The towering monstrosity hadn't seen a paint-brush in a decade and would almost certainly make an architect flinch.

Glory was accustomed to the two flights of stairs to her apartment and ran up them with ease. The dim light from a single bare bulb in the hall cast deep shadows as she shoved her key into the lock. It stuck as it always did. After wiggling it vigorously, she gave the door a firm kick.

It swung open onto a large cluttered room. The furniture looked as though it had been gathered from the attics of families of every social level imaginable. Dropping her worn shoulder bag to a trunk doubling as coffee table, she stretched luxuriously, her movements smooth and supple, resembling those of a young, healthy cat.

"How come so late?"

Swinging around, Glory smiled as a short, slightly stocky woman walked into the room. The long purple T-shirt she wore combined with her short shaggy brown hair to give her a wacky, waifish look.

"Dr. Morrison had to leave early," Glory said as she sat on the couch, propping her feet up on the trunk. "So I had to handle everything myself. Then just as I was getting ready to close down the clinic for the day, a boy came in with his arm sliced up."

Addie Howard pushed her round-framed glasses back on her freckled nose with one finger. "Knife wounds? And you were there with him by yourself? Glory, that's dumb. I don't suppose you called the police to report it?"

Glory smiled. "Didn't have time," she murmured drowsily, then opened both eyes to glance at her friend. "You won't believe what happened. Remember last month when Daddy summoned me so urgently?"

"The new man?"

Glory nodded. "He showed up today during my

lunch break while I was playing softball with some kids. I can't get him out of my hair. Two weeks ago the Houston thing, and now this."

"You didn't tell me you saw him in Houston."

She shrugged. "There was nothing to tell. He just showed up like the ghost of Christmas past at Tess Wollencott's charity bash." She shook her head. "I can't understand it. I've lived in Dallas for five years and have never seen hide nor hair of him in all this time; now all of a sudden he's popping up everywhere. It's spooky as hell."

"Sounds like some dates I've had," Addie said dryly. "The ones who have the personality and looks of an Irish potato are always so damn devoted. You never did tell me about him. What was his name—Spencer?"

Glory nodded, then leaned her head back, closing her eyes for a second as she called up a ready image of Alan Spencer. "Dark hair—not black, but a deep mahogany brown," she murmured. "He has this little scar on his cheek. When he smiles, it looks like some kind of freaked-out dimple, and when he frowns, it makes him look rather fierce, like a dark pirate." She drew in a deep breath. "He's tall, well-built, and looks like a cross between Sylvester Stallone and Robert Redford . . . not as meaty as Stallone, not as pretty as Redford." She sounded as if she were reciting memorized material when she continued to describe him. "He's intelligent, articulate, and has a kind of off-beat sense of humor that is intensely appealing." Glory opened her eyes, raised one brow, and glanced wryly at her friend. "An Irish potato?"

Addie whistled softly between her teeth. "Definitely not a potato. You've got me breathing hard just hearing about him. Since you didn't want him, why didn't you bring the leftovers home for me?"

"You know why. I've—"

She broke off as a young man, his bulk awesome, ambled across the room. Curly brown hair stuck out at odd angles from his round face. He was wearing nothing other than horn-rimmed glasses and yellow boxer shorts with gray kittens frolicking across them.

Both women watched as he walked to the refrigerator in the adjoining open kitchen. Pulling out the makings for the sandwich of all sandwiches, he began silently to assemble it. The architectural wonder grew larger and larger as they stared in fascination. Just when they thought catastrophe was imminent, he carried it to the living room, sat on the floor beside the coffee table, and began to eat.

"Booger," Addie said. "Are you awake?"

Raising his eyes from the sandwich, Arnold Schlumburger glanced around the room, then back to Addie. "I don't know. Do I have mayonnaise on my chin?" Both women nodded. "Then I'm awake." With that he continued to eat.

Addie rolled her eyes expressively at Glory before saying, "If this guy is as cute as you say, why didn't you at least make a date to meet him somewhere? He doesn't have to know where you live."

"Don't think I didn't consider it," she admitted.

"I thought about him all day at the clinic . . . and thought and thought," she added with a grin.

Addie's eyes widened. "Don't tell me Your Aloofness finally met a man who made her pulse beat faster? That must have shook you."

Was that what was wrong with her? Glory wondered with a puzzled frown. That first night, on the plane ride home, she had looked back over the evening—not without a little embarrassment—trying to figure out why she had overdone the turnoff. In the past, she had always been more subtle. Was she more attracted to Alan Spencer than she wanted to admit? Could that explain the weird, panicky sensation that had hit her the minute he walked into her father's study?

Glancing up, she found Addie watching her intently. "He must be something," her friend said quietly.

Glory shrugged casually, trying to rid her mind of memory of him. "He is, but he is also a complication I don't need right now. If I dated him, how long could I go on meeting him someplace else? And what about when I started breaking dates because I had to work? I told you he was intelligent . . . and I mean really sharp. He knew something wasn't right that first night. Another half hour and he probably would have had the whole thing figured out." She grinned suddenly. "But he wasn't about to stay around me for another thirty minutes." She shook her head. "Then he pops up in Houston and again today here in Dallas. He already knows I'm not Miss Dallas Deb. If I saw him again, how long would it be before Daddy found out everything? I can't take a chance on something like that happening."

"I think you made the right decision," Booger mumbled through a bite of pickle. "Who needs a guy who is rich, good-looking, and intelligent hanging around?" He chewed and swallowed noisily, then turned to Glory. "I wouldn't put too much stock in the impact he has obviously made on you. What we've got here is a classic case of male odorants that fired off receptors in your olfactory epithelia, and vice versa . . . pheromones as it were—even though they may not exist in humans. Of course we don't want them to exist, because that reminds us that we are, after all, only animals and—"

"Oh, for heaven's sake, Booger, shut up and eat your sandwich," Addie said, her voice repressive.

"I was only trying to explain what happened to her," he said, shrugging. "Chemical reaction is not to be sneered at. It happens to me all the time."

"What's going on?"

Everyone looked up as a beautiful, curvaceous blonde walked into the room. Her statuesque figure was inadequately covered by a baby blue sleep teddy, and she dragged the matching robe behind her as she walked, rubbing her eyes sleepily.

"For heaven's sake, Delilah," Addie said in disgust. "Put on your robe. Booger's glasses are beginning to fog up."

"I don't mind," he said courageously.

Delilah Jones pulled on the blue robe, tying it at her slender waist. "Why are you all sitting around at one in the morning?" she asked huskily. "Glory, don't you go on call tomorrow?"

Addie glanced at Glory. "Be sure and grab the top bunk," she said, her voice dry. "They always go to the bottom bunk in an emergency."

Glory didn't comment. Her eyes were trained on Delilah in wonderment. "Since when are you interested enough to remember my schedule?"

Delilah smiled. "I always remember when you have to stay over at the hospital because it means I can sleep in your room. Someone"—she glanced pointedly at Addie—"leaves the light on all night."

"*Someone* likes to be prepared when Dr. Auerbach asks a question," Addie said brusquely.

"*Someone*—" Delilah began.

"We were discussing the man Glory's father fixed her up with last month," Booger said, his placid voice bringing calm to the room. "And the fact that Glory can't see him again because her father might find out what she's doing."

Delilah sat on the edge of a sagging papasan chair. "I don't see why you can't just tell your father the truth." The blonde leaned forward to rest her chin in the palms of her hands. "I've heard a disgusting rumor that honesty is the best policy."

Addie snorted. "This comes from the girl who has stolen my best panty hose three days running."

Delilah ignored her. "I just can't see what the fuss is all about. Glory's father would buy Neiman's and give it to her wrapped in red tissue paper if she wanted it." Raising one arched eyebrow, she glanced at Glory. "You can't make me believe he would be angry with you."

Glory smiled sadly. How could she make them understand that it was not what her father would do to her, but what it would do to her father to find out? She would tell him . . . someday; when she had her medical license in her hand; when it was too late to try to talk her out of her decision; when he had no time to use his considerable influence on hospital boards. She inhaled deeply and slowly. And when she felt she was strong enough to witness the pain that would appear in his eyes when she told him that she was a doctor.

Glory glanced up to find the others staring at her sympathetically. They were good friends, all of them. It was still difficult for her to believe five such different people could live in relative harmony, but they had turned out to be the brothers and sisters Glory had never had.

She smiled. "Why isn't Mr. Moto out here? He always manages to get in his two cents worth."

"He's got a *hot date*," Delilah said, giving the last two words extra emphasis.

Glory shrugged. "So what else is new? One of these days he's going to run out of medical students to impress and start having withdrawal symptoms."

They heard a key in the lock, then the door was kicked enthusiastically. "Speak of the devil," Addie said with heavy sarcasm as a slender, dark-haired young man sauntered into the room.

"I hate to be the one to mention it, Jack," Addie said dryly, "but disco mania is dead."

Jack Takara, the last of the roommates, wore a green satin shirt open to the waist and black slacks that clung tightly to his trim hips and thighs. There was a devilish sparkle in his dark, almond-shaped eyes that were so appealing to female medical students.

Glory grinned. "I think you're telling the wrong person," she said, her voice teasing. "You need to tell those women who constantly drool all over him."

Jack walked on into the room. "What is this? Are you all waiting up for me? A plate of cookies and a glass of milk on the table would have been sufficient."

"We're discussing Glory's problems."

"You got problems, Glory? What's the matter, is Blumenthal still giving you a hard time? I could always use my influence as a respected resident to get you better treatment." He glanced at the other man in the room. "Kittens on your shorts, Booger? Get serious."

"It's not Blumenthal," Addie said. "It's her father. Today she ran into the last man her father summoned her to Austin to meet. She's afraid her father is going to find out what she's doing."

Jack lowered himself to the couch beside Glory. "The business date from last month? So what's bothering you? If you dumped this guy, what have you got to worry about?"

"I'm not worrying about him," Glory said. "I've run into him a couple of times. I guess I'm feeling guilty about keeping all this from Daddy. It seemed so simple in the beginning. All I had to do was go to school here in Dallas and fly home a couple of times a month. I was young and stupid . . . and maybe a little rebellious," she admitted reluctantly. "I thought if I could go to him as a licensed physician, I would be in a better position to convince him that this is right for me." She shook her head. "It's all been too easy until now. And Daddy didn't ask questions because he thought I was simply having a fling. But it's been almost *five years*."

Glory glanced around at her friends. "Why do you think he started this matchmaking thing? He's beginning to worry about me. Since I always manage to walk away from these men he brings home for me to meet, he—" She broke off, laughter filling her eyes.

"Come on, tell," Delilah urged.

Glory straightened her face, struggling to keep her voice bland as she said, "He's beginning to have doubts about my femininity."

They all stared at her with stunned expressions, then whoops of laughter broke the silence in the room. Booger rolled onto his side against the couch, causing alarming tremors in the aged piece of furniture as he shook with laughter. Wiping his eyes, he said. "You mean he thinks you're butch?"

Glory shook her head. "No, I think." she gasped, "that he thinks I'm—I'm a neuter . . . asexual."

Jack dropped his arm around her shoulders, giving her a squeeze. "He's obviously never seen you ogling Dr. Auerbach," he said, still chuckling.

"I don't!" Glory protested, then when every eye in the room turned on her with skepticism, she added, "Okay, maybe I ogle occasionally." She slid lower on the couch, brushing the hair from her forehead. "But you can see my problem. This is all getting more complicated than I had expected."

"Listen to a bit of Oriental wisdom, glorious Glory," said Jack—born and raised in Cincinnati, Ohio—"from the minute you're labeled *adult*, you're bombarded from all sides by choices. All you can do is pick one and stick to it . . . to the dismal end."

"Is that supposed to be sympathetic?"

"It's supposed to be the truth, which is more important than sympathy."

"But not nearly as comforting," she murmured as she stood up. "But you're right. The fact is, I started this charade for a good reason. The reason still exists, so the charade will too."

Five

Alan got out from his car and looked up at the glass-fronted building. It was one of a new breed of office complexes that were spreading the city of Dallas northward.

Alan's own building was closer to downtown, but he wasn't unfamiliar with this area. He often had meetings in one of these office buildings. But it wasn't business that brought him here today. This particular building housed the Dallas office of Wainwright, Inc. Alan was ready for answers.

His lips tightened. He had called Wainwright in Mexico, but the older man had just left on a three-day fishing trip. Alan had already waited a week. After the last encounter he didn't want to wait even three more days to find Glory. The people here would know her address.

He stepped off the elevator on the twelfth floor and walked briskly into the reception area. He didn't pause as he headed for the older woman behind the desk.

"Hello," he said, smiling his most charming smile. "It's Helen, isn't it?"

"Yes, that's right," she said, her expression alert. "Can I help you, Mr. Spencer?"

"You certainly can." He leaned against her desk, giving the feeling of intimacy. "Helen, I've got a little problem. Your boss asked me to keep in touch with his daughter, Glory, while he was in Mexico." He grinned in boyish embarrassment. "The thing is, Helen, I've lost her address, and I wondered if you could look it up for me."

"I'm sorry," she said, genuine regret in her answering smile. "I have strict orders not to give out Miss Wainwright's address. It's office policy."

He leaned closer. "I can understand that. But this is different. You know that Wainwright and I are business associates."

Her smile sliding away, she shook her head. "Orders are orders."

"Orders," Alan said contemptuously, emotion blinding him. "For heaven's sake, woman, you can give me the damn address. I'm Alan Spencer of Spencer-Houghton International."

Helen straightened the glasses on her nose and drew herself up taller. "I don't care if you're Ethelred the Unready," she said, staring at him stubbornly. "I don't give out Miss Wainwright's address."

"But—"

Alan broke off as he watched the light of battle grow in the woman's eyes. This would get him nowhere. He had botched it, but good. He faced rooms full of hostile businessmen with equanimity. He negotiated with shrewdness and finesse against cunning adversaries. Now, full of seething emotion, over anxious and acting like an adolescent, he'd blown it. He snorted in self-disgust.

He nodded a curt good-bye to Helen, turned on his heel, and walked back toward the elevator. When he pulled the Mercedes out of the parking lot, the squealing tires gave evidence of his frustration.

His lips were drawn in a tight line, his shoulders stiff as he joined the heavy noontime traffic on LBJ Freeway. When a car swerved across three lanes in front of him and he slammed on the brakes, he realized his reflexes were slower than usual.

Damn Glory, he thought in anger. He had to get his mind off her. He wanted to see her now. But he knew he would have to wait until Wainwright came home. Reason told him it couldn't be helped, but reason or no, Alan was not a man who was used to waiting, and he didn't like it one bit.

Glory leaned against the wall, flexing one foot then the other. She was tired, and she knew she looked it. Her own father would have had to look twice to recognize the girl who had had dinner with him and Alan Spencer three weeks earlier. Her hair was pulled back in a French braid; a stethoscope lay draped around her neck, a white coat covering her plain yellow slacks and blouse. There wasn't a trace of makeup on her face, and she smelled of rubbing alcohol.

She frowned as she always did when she thought of Alan, uncomfortable with how often that happened. It was ridiculous that she should still be thinking of him after so long. At times she would catch herself in the dangerous game of "what if." What if they had met under different circumstances? What if he were not an acquaintance of her father's? What if they just happened to meet again?

Always, she would push such thoughts away from her. If all those things were true, Glory knew she would still stay away from Alan Spencer. The next few months were crucial to her career. She couldn't afford a distraction, and there was no denying Alan was the most effective distraction she had met in a long, long while.

Straightening away from the rough wall, Glory glanced around the antiseptic area. She had been assigned to emergency room duty three days earlier, and already it had taken its toll on her.

Glory had never let anyone guess the terrors ER held for her. Nightmare time. Pulling OR duty wasn't nearly as bad. In surgery they were putting people back together—an orderly fixing. ER was unscheduled but inevitable horror. Automobile accidents, job screw-ups, and family quarrels brought people of all ages into ER with parts missing and life being extinguished through systematic violence.

ER was affecting her even more this time. She had just spent six days on call and, although she was tired to the point of exhaustion, she was looking forward to being freed from prison.

The worst part of being on call was being away from her friends. She laughed softly. They were all a little crazy, but she loved them and missed their craziness when she was away from them. Only last night Booger had another birthday.

None of the roommates questioned the fact that he had as many as ten or fifteen birthdays a year. When he announced another birthday, they simply wrapped whatever was available in bathroom tissue or leftover Christmas paper and had an instant party. Ritualistically he would exclaim over each chipped cup and half-empty box of macaroni as though it had been shipped in from Mount Olympus especially for him.

Booger's birthdays always coincided suspiciously with low spots in the lives of individual roommates. If one of them was crossed in love or made a mistake in front of staff, Booger had a birthday. The day before, Addie fouled up a spinal tap and had been flogging herself unmercifully . . . so Booger had announced another birthday.

Glory chuckled softly as she thought of her friends. She considered anyone who wanted to be a doctor slightly cracked—herself included. But for as long as Glory could remember, this had been her dream.

Some dream, she thought, sighing wearily. What fool would yearn for controlled chaos? And in the midst of all the confusion, one thing was clear. Interns were expendable.

To the medical student, interns had obtained a

kind of Nirvana because the rigors of med school were behind them. But it was the general opinion of the hospital staff that an intern's IQ was just one step above that of a self-sealing envelope. Any dirty, annoying, repulsive job that was too complicated for a medical student was done by an intern. Someone in the medical system—most likely someone totally removed from actual medicine—believed in trial by fire. If a doctor could make it through internship, then, by George, he deserved that medical license.

For the moment the emergency room was blessedly quiet, and Glory headed for the coffeepot. It had been a rough morning and the caffeine seemed essential to her physical and mental well-being.

"Wainwright! Jones!"

The call from the ER resident brought Glory up short. "Hell," she muttered, too softly to be heard because she valued her life. She should have known she would never make it all the way to the coffeepot. She met Delilah at one of the partitions set up for patient examinations.

"An accident in the wire factory," Delilah explained briskly. "This one was half-hypnotized by watching the wire go through the die and decided to reach out to touch it. He wasn't wearing his gloves."

"Oh, great," Glory said in resignation, knowing what was coming next. The wire factory four blocks away sent injured workers to the ER on a regular basis. "And then he found to his surprise he couldn't let go."

"Right," Delilah said. "It grabbed him and wrapped him around a spool of hot wire. If he hadn't been dragged across the automatic kill switch, it probably would have thrown him into a steel beam. Remember that one last month?"

Glory didn't want to remember the man who would probably be in a coma for the rest of his life. He was on the list of things she tried very hard to forget.

"As it is," Delilah continued, "he has second-degree burns on his chest and the inside of his arm."

"The clean-up is going to hurt like hell," Glory murmured, then glanced warily at Delilah. "How big is he?"

"Big enough to sit on both of us."

Glory let out a slow breath. When a grown man had pain inflicted upon him, he was liable to get a little touchy. More than once Glory had left ER with bruises. "Okay," she said. "Which one of us is going to convince him to let us strap him down?"

Delilah smoothed back her blond hair. "Let me have a shot at it. Most big guys are puppy dogs underneath."

Delilah's magic worked once again, but as they cleaned the man's burns, Glory began to wonder if the straps would hold. It seemed like hours before they had finished treating him and left him in the care of a nurse. They were both exhausted, but Glory looked it. Annoyingly Delilah still appeared as cool and fresh as she had when they left the apartment that morning.

This time they came within three feet of the coffeepot before they heard the inevitable call.

"Wainwright!"

Glory moaned and closed her eyes.

"Go ahead and get coffee," Delilah said. "I'll cover for you."

Glory shook her head. "No, I'll go." She raised her eyes heavenward. "Someone is testing my dedication. I don't want to fall short."

Straightening her back, Glory walked to the cubicle Dr. Blumenthal had indicated. With brisk movements she pulled aside the curtain, then almost stumbled when she saw the patient. A small boy smiled irresistibly at her. On the top of his head, like a crown, was a blue plastic potty. Beside him, his mother smiled stiffly, her arms crossed, her expression frustrated and faintly defiant, as if to say, "You try to do something with him."

More than an hour had passed before Glory finally managed to get to the coffeepot. Delilah was there again—or still—lounging against the wall as she flirted with a personable young doctor. When she saw Glory, she left him immediately to join her friend.

"Steve tells me you had an interesting case," she said, her green eyes laughing. "Something to write up in the medical journals." She leaned closer. "Tell me, Dr. Wainwright, how did you bring about this miraculous recovery?"

"I slapped on some Vaseline and unscrewed him," she said dryly as she flexed her back. It felt stiff. The little boy hadn't turned his head over to her willingly. "Why did we decide to become doctors, Delilah? Doesn't it strike you as a rather stupid move right now?"

Delilah shrugged elegantly. "You decided to become a doctor because you feel in your well-heeled gut that you can help people. I decided to become a doctor because once I get through all this nonsense, I will not only be making a lot of money, I will—if all goes as planned—marry a doctor who makes lots of money. Which means I will divert something extremely unpleasant—poverty with a capital P." She shook back her hair in a casual movement. "You've never been there, Glory, but let me tell you, being poor is boring as hell. And you know I always managed to avoid being bored."

Glory stared hard at her friend. At times she found herself falling for Delilah's carefree good-time-girl act, then the blonde would do or say something that would pull Glory up short. The act was so polished, it was easy to forget that underneath the smooth exterior, intense wars were raging. Sometimes Glory caught a glimpse of loneliness so deep, it made her ache for her friend. The blonde had never once volunteered details about her background, and the roommates respected her reserve. Delilah was motivated by things Glory couldn't understand but respected nevertheless.

After they had had a cup of coffee, Delilah and Glory walked out of the lounge and back into ER. Seconds after they entered the area, the double exterior doors burst open, signaling trouble. Stretchers and emergency medical technicians began pouring into the room.

Glory grabbed the arm of a passing nurse. "What happened?" she asked.

"A car pileup on LBJ," the nurse said before moving away hurriedly.

"Wainwright! Jones!"

And it all began again. All available doctors worked frantically until the worst cases had been diagnosed and taken away. As always, Glory shut off the side of her brain that told her to be horrified and worked feverishly on the cases assigned to her. Time expanded and contracted simultaneously while she was totally absorbed in her work. A curious kind of tunnel vision took over, and the world consisted, not of a patient, but of a specific wound. The objectivity had been difficult to acquire, but was necessary in order to tend to the job at hand.

"Wainwright," Dr. Blumenthal said curtly as Glory finished suturing a leg wound, "take care of the man in A. Here's the chart. Contusions and abrasions. Possible concussion."

Grabbing the chart, Glory whipped strands of black hair from her eyes and made her way to cubicle A. Stepping through the curtain, she glanced at the chart. "Well, now, Mr.—" she began, then glanced up quickly at the man standing beside the examining table.

"Spencer," he said softly. "Alan Spencer."

Six

"Oh, sh—"

"My thoughts exactly," Alan said dryly, interrupting her. He stared at her openly, shaking his head in exasperation. "Now, why didn't I guess you'd be here?" He laughed shortly. "It's your fault I'm here in the first place."

"My fault?" She looked confused and very wary.

"Never mind," he said, unwilling to admit his mind had been on her instead of on the idiots inhabiting the freeway.

His gaze drifted over the white coat, the stethoscope draped around her neck. He wasn't as surprised at finding her here as he probably should have been. Annoyed, frustrated, and exasperated, but not surprised. And beneath all those emotions was a pleased feeling, a kind of satisfaction that the missing piece of a puzzle had finally fallen into place.

Her attempt to pull herself together was visible, and, almost, he felt sorry for her . . . almost. He had spent too many uncomfortable nights because of this woman to be entirely sympathetic.

Her dismay was almost comical as she said slowly, "Mr. Spencer—"

"Alan," he corrected her, continuing his examination. "You're a doctor."

"Yes . . . at least I'm an intern," she said, studying her feet as intensely as he was studying her. "I have my degree in medicine but not my license."

"An intern." He shook his head. He picked up one of her hands and stared down at it. "Very capable-looking hands," he murmured. "I would trust myself to these hands. Yes, this is much better," he said, inhaling slowly. "I should have looked at your hands instead of listening to your nonsense. Not an android, not a party girl, not even a Little Leaguer . . . a doctor," he added in satisfaction.

Glory stared down at her hand resting in his. She couldn't think when he touched her. Blinking in confusion, she heard Dr. Blumenthal's voice outside the cubicle. Paling slightly, she stepped closer. "Mr.—Alan," she said urgently. "I realize I owe you some sort of explanation, but right now I've got to take care of your injuries."

After a moment he said, "Be my guest."

She cleared her throat. With an effort she pushed aside all her emotions so the doctor could take over. "Your chart says there are possible head injuries. Can you show me where?" He indicated a dark spot on his temple. "Yes, there's a bruise," she said briskly. "If you'll sit on the table, I'll take a look at it."

Instead of sitting on the end of the table where the step-up was, he simply slid onto the side, leaving her in the awkward position of having to get close to the wound without getting too close to the man.

"You can't possibly see it from that distance," he said, and Glory could hear the amusement in his voice. He pulled her closer until she was pressed up against his hard thigh. "Now, Doc, tell me, is this going to ruin my good looks? Will I ever go on the stage again?"

"It's not large, but it's in a bad place," she murmured, ignoring his teasing questions as she shined a light in his eyes, checking the pupil reaction. "Did you lose consciousness at all?"

"No, but I did get a little dizzy when I saw you again," he said softly.

He shifted his position, and suddenly, somehow, Glory was standing between his legs, his hands on her hips as he looked into her eyes. She had never been in a situation quite like this; there were no guidelines for correct behavior in this instance. She knew she should get on with the examination, but she felt paralyzed by his nearness, by the feel of his thighs pressing against her.

"What do you think it means, Doc?" Alan asked, his voice low and husky. "Could the dizziness be a sign of something serious?"

Glory could feel her heart pounding in her chest and the racing of the blood in her veins, but she refused to give in to the sensation. She was a professional, she told herself, and could work under any conditions.

"Was there any nausea following the blow?" Was that her voice? she wondered. Why did it sound so sensuous, even to her own ears?

"No," he answered, the word low and husky. "No nausea, no blurred vision, no headache . . . you have the most incredible eyes I have ever seen."

She cleared her throat nervously. Reaching up, she gently brushed the hair from his temple. "I'll need to clean this up with antiseptic, then . . . then we'll get on to the cut on your arm."

Alan heard the words, but they didn't penetrate. Her fingers on his face caused his blood to throb strangely in his neck. He was close enough to her to see the fine texture of her skin.

"Alan, if you'll let me go, I'll get the antiseptic."

Alan simply stared. The world receded as he became enthralled by the way her lips moved. The delicacy of her features amazed him. There was an Old World fineness about her, a sensual elegance.

"A Persian rose," he murmured. "Straight out of an antique book of fairy tales."

Glory drew in a swift breath, then almost flinched at the pleasure the scent of him brought. Was Booger right? Was there a chemical reaction between them? Was that what made her want to get closer, and even closer?

She felt his hands tighten on her hips and her eyes met his just in time to see him leaning toward her. She could have avoided the kiss, but she didn't. Instead, she moved into it. Then she stood perfectly still as his lips moved across hers, tasting and testing.

His hands pressed her closer, moving her against his arousal, and the feeling flooded her with pleasure, shocking her. Think of it clinically, she thought urgently. Examine what was happening in detail and it would go away. It was simply—she moaned as his lips found the hollow of her throat—it was simply blood engorging certain areas, making them more sensitive to touch. Dammit, that's all it was.

But the analysis didn't work. The picture she had painted was too erotic to be clinical. Shoving her arms against his chest, Glory backed away from him, her eyes wide and wary.

"Glory," he said hoarsely.

She shook her head frantically. Where was her objectivity? This was no doctor-patient relationship. This was a drugging, enervating experiment in sensuality. And Glory simply couldn't allow it to continue. It was even worse than the other times. She had to get away from the addictive nearness of him.

"Excuse me," she whispered, then ducked quickly through the curtain.

Holding her trembling hands tightly to her sides, she walked away from the cubicle. She drew in a deep breath when she saw Delilah emerge from another examining room.

"Delilah," she said, straining to keep her voice normal. "I'm a little shaky." She smiled. "Probably from missing lunch. The man in A . . ." Frowning, she glanced over her shoulder toward the cubicle.

"Don't sweat it," Delilah said. "I'll take care of him while you have a break."

"Thanks, Dee," Glory murmured, smoothing her dark hair back with a hand that still shook slightly. "You're a real pal."

The blonde smiled. "While that's not my ultimate ambition, I'll accept it for now." She gave Glory's arm a comforting squeeze. "Don't take everything so seriously. You've been forgetting lately that you're only mortal like the rest of us."

Glory smiled weakly, then made her way to the lounge. The small room was blessedly empty. Collapsing on the vinyl couch, she leaned her head back and closed her eyes. But when Alan's face loomed in her mind, she opened them wide again.

She couldn't escape from the expression on his face . . . or how she had felt when she had touched him. Where was her famous aloofness? There was something there, something between them that made her nerve ends tingle in awareness.

What on earth was she going to do? She couldn't even think straight; how was she ever going to straighten out the mess she found herself smack in the middle of? Alan knew the truth now. Not only was there a very real possibility that her father would learn everything from someone other than herself, but that someone else was affecting her in a way she had never been affected before.

Oh, what a tangled web we weave, she thought wryly. She had known that first night that Alan lived in Dallas. But Dallas was a big, sprawling city. She had never imagined she would keep running into him this way. It had seemed a safe bet that they would never see each other again.

She could manage her emotions, she told herself bracingly. She had always been strong in that area. But what was she going to do about her father?

She stood and began pacing the small floor. If her father found out from a virtual stranger that she was a doctor, she had only herself to blame. She should have faced him years ago. But somehow the time had never seemed right. After her mother's death, they had grown very close, but then after Uncle Peter died—

She pushed the thought of her paternal uncle away. Uncle Peter was the reason she found it impossible to tell her father the truth.

Glancing at the clock, Glory realized she would have to leave the safety of the lounge. She couldn't hide all day. Although the emergency of the freeway accident was over, there would be others. That fact was guaranteed.

When she made her way back to ER, Alan was gone. But her relief at his departure didn't keep her from noticing the strange looks she got from Delilah. Through the rest of their shift the blond woman watched Glory closely, her expression revealing her feelings of concern mingled with curiosity.

Delilah was sharp, Glory told herself. The blonde didn't miss much. She would have realized as soon as she saw Alan's name who he was. And Glory knew her friend was dying to question her about what had happened in the examination room, but

Glory wasn't ready to discuss it yet. She had to get it straight in her own mind first.

As soon as their shift was over, Glory slipped away. Rather than going straight home, she headed for a small park near the apartment. She needed time to think.

The wind had an unexpected chill in it, causing her to wrap her sweater closer as she walked around the park. She noticed with surprise that the leaves were beginning to turn. How could fall have come to Dallas without her being aware of it?

Shaking her head ruefully, she admitted that she had been so wrapped up in her work, the leaves could have turned neon pink and she wouldn't have noticed.

A solitary jogger moved past her, his breathing rhythmic. Always the joggers. Their presence never failed to reassure her somehow. They reaffirmed her faith in the human spirit. She firmly believed that on the day after nuclear destruction, while walking through the rubble, any survivors would be overtaken by correctly attired joggers.

Passing a group of children, she smiled as she watched them swarming across a sand moat that surrounded a castle built of tires and two-by-fours. Worker bees, she thought in a moment of whimsy, moving in and out of a hive, the flow continuous. Some were carrying in nectar and pollen, some spreading royal jelly about the individual cells, stopping occasionally to rub antennae.

Their voices blended with the sound of going-home traffic. "Boys go to Jupiter to get more stupider. Girls go to Mars to get more candy bars."

Inhaling deeply, she let the normalcy of her surroundings soothe her. Things weren't as bad as she imagined them to be. She would find a way out of this problem.

Okay, smartass, she thought morosely, *and how do you propose to do that?*

Alan was one of her father's business associates. He would surely mention the fact that he had seen her at the hospital to her father. Glory rubbed her throbbing temples. She had no idea how often the two men saw each other, but sooner or later it had to come out.

She closed her eyes, feeling a sharp pain in the region of her heart as she imagined her father's face when he heard what Alan had to tell him, and when he finally realized it was the truth.

Oh, Daddy, she thought in despair, *I didn't want to hurt you.*

Opening her eyes, she tightened her jaw. She couldn't let this thing overcome her. Her father was in Mexico and wouldn't be back for more than two weeks. In that time she would make sure Alan understood the situation. If her father had to know the truth now before she was ready, then Glory would have to make sure the truth came from her. It was the only way.

The pain that was in the future for her and for her father was almost a visual image for her, and she felt weak with the futility of it all. But she was caught up in a flow of events that had moved beyond her control.

Suddenly she pulled herself up short. Since when had she become a defeatist? She must be more tired than she had realized. She was a survivor. The odds on her getting into medical school and then making it through without her father's help proved it. More than once she had been down to her last can of tomato soup . . . but she had survived and she could survive this.

She inhaled deeply. Adrenaline began pumping through her. She felt almost invincible. She was one tough cookie, she assured herself with a laugh.

"Come on, world," she said aloud. "Do your worst. I can take it."

Almost as soon as the words were out, a gust of wind picked up a cloud of sand and blew it into her face. Wrinkling her nose, she muttered, "You didn't have to take me so seriously, for heaven's sakes," and turned to walk to her car, unwilling to press her luck.

Ten minutes later, when she walked into the apartment, everyone was there. Booger was putting together a model airplane; Jack was flexing his biceps as he watched his reflection in the window; Delilah sat beside Booger, painting her toenails a blinding shade of purple.

Addie stood on her head in the corner of the room with a murder mystery held close to her nose. When she saw Glory, there was a fanning of short legs, and she awkwardly regained an upright position. "Where have you been?" she said brusquely. "We've been worried sick."

"Sorry, mother," Glory said, giving a small smile.

Jack glanced away from his image. "Gloriosky, Glory, you look like hell."

"That's funny, I feel like hell," Glory said, her voice dry. "These things must come in pairs."

"Dee told us the blind date showed up at the hospital today," Booger said as he concentrated on attaching a bit of wing to the *Spirit of St. Louis*. "What happened?"

Glory glanced away from her friends, unwilling to pull them in what was, after all, a dilemma only to herself.

"I think he was in an accident on the freeway," she said, keeping her tone light as she walked to the kitchen.

"Come on," Addie said. "What happened? Delilah said you were a little hyper after he left."

Glory pulled the pop top from a can of diet soda and turned around, sighing as she leaned against the counter. "Obviously he knows I'm a doctor now," she said quietly. "I don't know what he's going to do with the information, because I ducked out before we could discuss it." She smiled weakly. "But I don't think I can hold on to the hope that he won't mention it to my father." She shrugged wearily. "As they say in the movies, the jig is up."

Moving to the big double window overlooking an unkempt garden, Glory stared beyond the yard. For the past four years she had seen this view daily. She could still remember the day she had found the apartment. At that time there had been only two roommates, Addie and a nursing student with flaming red hair. They had each had a bedroom to themselves, and the place had been quieter. The student had become a nurse and left, and gradually the other three had come to join them.

Each was so different from the others, but together the five of them seemed to mesh into something resembling a family.

She felt a shudder of cold run through her, cold that represented change. Even if she could get through the trauma of telling her father the truth, her life would never be the same. George Wainwright had never settled for anything less than what he considered the best for his only daughter. How would he view this curious group of people?

Leaning her head against the window, Glory realized she had more than one fight ahead of her. Cowards never prosper, she thought wryly. Maybe the adage was for cheaters, but she was sure it worked equally well for cowards. If she had faced her father years ago, none of this would be happening.

But if she had told him at the beginning, would she even have made it through medical school?

She knew what power her father wielded. He was a wonderful, caring father, but he was also a man who showed his love and concern by manipulation. And Glory was not the only one who would feel his power. One by one, these people, her friends, would feel it personally, and one by one, they would leave her. Suddenly she felt the strength she had found in the park slip away from her. One minute a lion, the next a lamb.

"What are you going to do?" Delilah's voice came from directly behind Glory.

Turning around, she blinked away unexpected tears. She might as well prepare them. Biting her lip, she tried to form an answer. Then suddenly she glanced at each face, and the expressions there stopped her.

Glory's small stature usually brought out a protective instinct in people. But with this group she had been immediately accepted as the strong person she was. She was the one they came to with their individual problems. They had never seen her cry. In their faces she saw anger and pain and indignation, all on her behalf. The caring in the room made her want to break down and really cry.

Booger cleared his throat. "All right, what we need to do is figure out a plan. Come on, Glorious Glory, sit down and we'll talk. We're beginning to look like a high school production of Macbeth."

Laughing brokenly, she moved to sit on the couch. Booger was right. She was letting it get out of hand. If only she weren't so blasted tired.

"You obviously feel this Alan Spencer is some kind of threat," Delilah said quietly. "Could it be that you're overestimating his power?"

She shook her head. "I'm not overestimating Alan, but I could be overestimating my importance. He may simply forget he saw me today and say nothing about it."

She stared down at her hands, remembering the intensity of feeling that flowed between them every time they met, remembering the look in his dark eyes when he kissed her. No, he definitely wouldn't forget.

"How long is your father going to be in Mexico?" Jack asked.

"Just a bit over two more weeks."

"Okay, then we've got two weeks to figure something out." He reached out to tweak her nose. "Don't look so woebegone, kid. There is no reason to let this man force you into doing something you don't want to do. We'll come up with something. Don't we always? Athos, Porthos, Aramis, D'Artagnan, and Moe—remember? When that visiting radiologist started stalking you, didn't we fix it?"

Glory shot him a skeptical glance from the corner of her eye. "You put Super Glue on the handle of his coffee cup."

He nodded smugly. "And didn't it take his mind off his bulging britches?"

She laughed, feeling her spirits lighten. A burden shared. "What are you proposing? Somehow I don't think Super Glue is the answer this time."

He shrugged. "I don't know, but don't anticipate disaster. Just stop worrying, because we'll fix it." He turned to look at the other man in the room. "Come on, Einstein, use that overrated brain of yours and figure out how to get Glory out of this mess."

Booger frowned. "Ask me for something simple . . . like Fermat's principle," he said dryly. He raised two fingers to his temple. "Wait—wait, I'm getting a flash. I've got it. All we have to do is prove that he's been passing information to the Russians and his word is ferret feces. Ooor," he said, dragging the word out interminably, "we could drug his imported coffee . . . keep him disoriented. Or"—his listeners groaned at the word—"we could kidnap him and lock him in the basement with the spiders and peach preserves until Glory passes her exams."

Punching him in the arm, Glory laughed in genuine enjoyment as she imagined her friends trying to tackle Alan Spencer. As much as she loved her friends, she would have to put her money on Alan. He had a mental and physical strength that he didn't bother to hide.

After Booger's suggestions, the ridiculous propositions for getting Glory out of her scrape came fast and furious. She was leaning against Jack, giggling helplessly, when someone knocked on the door of the apartment.

"You're all totally useless," she told the room at large as Addie made her way to the door. "And I really don't know what I would do without you."

"You would degenerate into a depressingly normal human being," Booger said, nodding his head sagely. "I've seen signs of it in you before and, I can tell you, I've been more than a little disturbed by it. If we weren't around to give you a diversity of viewpoints—the outré, the obscene, the disgusting, the macabre—you would probably become"— he shuddered dramatically—"*sane.*"

"You—" she began, then stopped abruptly.

In rigid resignation Glory turned her head as she heard a voice she would never mistake, never forget.

"I'm Alan Spencer," the man at the door said. "I'm looking for Gloria Wainwright."

Seven

Slowly Glory rose to her feet, aware that the same tension gripping her also affected her roommates. Addie glanced frantically over her shoulder, clearly unsure of what her next move should be.

Shrugging, Glory walked to the door and opened it wider when Addie stepped aside. Alan was standing in the hall, looking out of place against the faded wallpaper. She met his eyes hesitantly. "Oh, Lord," she said hoarsely, inhaling deeply before she blurted out, "What are you doing here? I mean . . . what do you want?"

Leaning against the doorjamb, he raised one heavy eyebrow. "Short and to the point," he murmured wryly. "I want peace on earth, an end to world hunger, and a good five-cent cigar . . . but right now I'll settle for an introduction." He nodded toward the people behind her.

Brushing her hair back, she moved to the side,

allowing him to enter the room. "Sure," she said brightly. "Why not? These are my roommates. Addie Howard this is Alan Spencer." Addie nodded slowly, studying Alan's face closely. Glory waved a hand toward the two men in the room. "Arnold Schlumburger and Jack Takara."

Booger pushed his glasses back with one finger, staring at Alan as though he were under a microscope. Jack simply flexed his muscles. Glory almost laughed. The gesture was probably intended to be threatening, but instead made him look twitchy.

Delilah shifted slightly in her chair, effectively drawing attention away from the men.

"And this is Delilah Jones," Glory said.

"Yes, Delilah and I have met," Alan said, smiling. "Hello again."

Delilah cocked an eyebrow, her smile of recognition detached. "Hello."

"Come in and sit down, Mr. Spencer," Booger said, his voice affable.

Alan glanced at each inhabitant of the room, his expression puzzled. Then he shifted his gaze back to Glory in inquiry.

Rubbing the palms of her hands on her slacks, she said, "Yes, of course, won't you sit down?" She moved into the room and scooped up a pile of lingerie from the only comfortable chair they owned.

"Now," Booger said when they were all seated, "tell me what it's like to be rich."

Alan laughed. "It's like being poor with nicer furniture and fancier food."

"Oh, sure," Jack said skeptically.

"I think Alan means that money doesn't change what's inside you," Glory volunteered, still holding the bundle of lingerie tightly.

"It would me," Booger said. "I'd have lots of steak and lobster inside me instead of tuna. There's something emasculating about tuna casserole."

"Jeez, Booger," Addie said, "can't you forget your stomach just for once?"

"Can I help it if I need a lot of protein to fuel my enormous brain?" he said loftily.

Jack snorted indelicately. "Don't you mean your enormous bulk?"

"Leave Booger alone," Delilah said, her voice stern. "You act like he's grossly overweight. I happen to think he's very attractive."

Booger leaned his head against her, his eyes adoring. "I think I love you," he said. "How do you feel about short, meaningless affairs?" He wiggled his eyebrows. "I'll show you my tattoo."

Alan laughed, then glanced at Glory. She was staring at a pink bra in her lap, looking oddly ill at ease in her own apartment. Lord, she was beautiful, he thought, his gaze tracing the lines of her face. But this time he wouldn't be seduced by her. This time he would get some answers. Suddenly, as though she felt his gaze on her, she glanced up.

"Could I buy you a cup of coffee?" he asked softly. When she hesitated, he added, "I really think we need to talk, Glory."

She stared at him for a moment, then nodded her head. "Yes, you're right."

Standing, she dropped the pile of laundry into the chair and pushed a lock of hair from her brow.

Alan smiled. It was always the same lock of hair. He liked the way it fell onto her forehead in a cocky, off-center curl.

"Alan and I are going for a cup of coffee," Glory announced to her friends. "We won't be long." When Jack looked as though he might protest, she shook her head slightly, warning him off. This was something she needed to do. She might as well get it over with now.

Moments later in the car, Alan asked, "Is it my imagination, or did I sense a little hostility back there?"

A smile quirked at her lips. "I'm afraid they're overprotective where I'm concerned."

"Overprotective?" he repeated, deep grooves appearing between his brows. "Do I look like someone you would need protection from?"

She sighed. "As I said today at the hospital, it's complicated."

And getting more so by the minute, Alan thought wryly, but he wasn't going to press her. Not yet.

Within minutes they reached a small coffee shop. Glory looked around as they entered and made their way to a table in the corner. It was small and homey, a good place to talk. She was glad he had chosen a place like this. She felt grubby and was sure she looked worse than she felt. Glancing up, she found him staring at her.

"Aren't you going to ask how I found out where you live?" he asked.

She shrugged, smiling slightly. "I'm George

Wainwright's daughter, remember? Who knows better what power and money can accomplish?"

He frowned. "Actually I asked a friend on the hospital board to look up your address for me. You almost make me feel guilty that I didn't bribe someone to get it."

She laughed softly. "I'm sorry, force of habit." She glanced down at her hands, bit her lip, then looked up again. "I suppose you think it's a little . . . well, odd that my father didn't tell you that I'm a doctor?"

"Now that you mention it," he said, grinning, "I guess it did strike me as a bit peculiar, but since I've met you, peculiar seems to be the norm, so I didn't spend too much time worrying about it. And, of course, it's really none of my business what you do."

She let out a long sigh of relief and smiled brilliantly, taking his breath away. "I'm very glad to hear you say that because the truth is I would rather you didn't mention it to my father."

Glancing down at the coffee cup, he said, "Your father is a pretty sharp man. Are you sure he doesn't know what you're doing?"

She shook her head. "I'm positive. I made very sure that he wouldn't find out. I chose Dallas for my training because I knew he wouldn't visit me here. I used my own money for medical school because I didn't want to explain the expense and . . . and because I didn't think it was right to use his money for something he would disapprove of. The money barely lasted, but I made it." She couldn't keep the pride from her voice. "Now I'm making a salary—well, almost a salary," she added, her eyes sparkling with amusement, "and I'm supporting myself."

"You said he would disapprove of your being a doctor," Alan said. "You're an adult; is his approval really so important?"

She frowned. "I'm not afraid of annoying my father," she said softly. "I just don't want to hurt him."

"Hurt him?"

She looked uncomfortable. "It's a personal matter."

"Yes, of course," he said. "I didn't mean to sound nosy. I'm sure you'll work it out as you see fit." He caught her gaze and added softly, "But don't you think you'd feel more comfortable if you told him? It must have been a little awkward going through this ruse."

"I'm going to tell him . . . eventually," she said, her voice slightly defensive. "I just want to wait until the time is right." She leaned closer. "Alan, you won't tell him, will you? I mean, would you make a conscious effort not to let it slip out when you're talking to him?"

Alan studied her face as she talked so earnestly. "God sure knew what he was doing when he put you together," he murmured softly.

Color rose in her cheeks, and Glory pulled back. She had shoved the incident in the hospital to the far reaches of her mind, which was why his statement took her by surprise. She merely stared at him blankly.

"Don't pull away," he said, leaning closer,

urgency appearing in his dark eyes. "Look, I know we haven't known each other long. I mean, we're not exactly intimate acquaintances . . . and yet we are. Don't you feel it, too . . . this thing between us? I don't know what to call it; I just know it's there, has been there since that first night."

For a moment she looked confused, then she said slowly, "Booger says it's pheromones or chemical reaction or something like that." She grinned. "Booger has a theory to fit any situation."

"Then you do feel it," he said, his relief obvious.

Lifting her head, she met his eyes. "I admit there's some basic physical attraction, but is that really so wonderful . . . so rare?"

Reaching out, he laid a gentle hand against her cheek. "Do you really think that's all there is to it, Glory?" he asked softly.

Glory's eyes drifted shut. There it was again, she thought disjointedly, that peculiar sensation. It was as though their cells had merged, as though his hand had become a part of her, as though his blood were flowing in her veins. How could she fight something that felt absolutely inevitable?

Pulling away from him, she drew in a deep, shaky breath.

He studied her face. "Why are you fighting so hard, Glory? If this thing between us means nothing, why can't you take it out and examine it in the light?"

She didn't know how to answer him. She had no good or logical reason why she couldn't just go with the flow of her emotions. It was some basic instinct, some inner voice saying, "Careful, there's danger here."

"Alan," she began hesitantly.

He shook his head before she could even begin an explanation. "No, don't say anything." His smile was self-mocking. "I'm badgering you; I know I am, but to tell you the truth, the whole thing has me baffled. I've never run across anything like you."

Glory giggled. She couldn't help it. When he raised a brow in inquiry, she said, "You make me sound like a dead skunk in the road."

Chuckling, he shook his head. "How can I carry on a serious conversation when you say things like that? I wish I had more time to explore your mind; I have a feeling it would be quite an adventure."

She bit her lip to hold back a smile, but when he muttered, "A dead skunk?" she burst out laughing.

Alan gazed at Glory in pleased silence, fascinated by the sapphire sparkle in her eyes. He finally knew the truth about her. He should be able to forget the whole thing now. But he knew he wouldn't. He knew the truth of her life, but he didn't yet know why she affected him the way she did. He hadn't yet divined why he was so drawn to her.

Without conscious intent he moved closer and suddenly his hand was on her chin, bringing her face to his. As if by magic, the laughter in her eyes died away and was replaced by the beckoning depths he had seen that first night.

Their lips met softly, tentatively, and Alan was attacked by the strangest sensation. It wasn't just that there was a rightness about her mouth against his; it was more that he felt right in him-self, as though she had somehow made him more complete.

For one beautiful moment Glory rode with the wave of tactile beauty the kiss brought. Then, with no warning, she felt afraid. Pulling back, she opened her eyes wide. "You—" she gasped breathlessly.

"Glory," he said, his voice urging her to come back.

Standing, she shook her head frantically. "You shouldn't do things like that. We came here just to talk." She rubbed her hands on her thighs nerv-ously. "You never did promise not to tell my father. Am I supposed to bribe you not to tell. Is that what all this was about?"

Alan stood, frowning. "Glory," he said again, clearly puzzled.

She backed away from him. "I don't play those games. Go ahead and tell Daddy. You can tell the President and his whole Cabinet for all I care."

Turning, she rushed away from the table and out of the café, leaving Alan to stare after her in bewilderment.

Glory climbed the last flight of stairs slowly. Instead of going into the apartment, she turned and sat on the top step. Closing her eyes, she relived every humiliating moment of the scene in the café. She had really done it this time.

"Glory?"

Turning around, she saw Addie and Delilah

coming out of the apartment together. Delilah was obviously dressed for a date, while Addie wore her usual overalls.

"What are you doing out here?" Addie asked.

"Thinking," she said, resting her chin in her hands. "Wondering why I do such stupid things."

Delilah moved to sit beside her. "I take it the talk with Spencer didn't go too well," she said.

"The understatement of the year," Glory said, her voice disgruntled. "I made an ass of myself."

Delilah sighed in exasperation. "Haven't you listened to any of my lectures? How many times have I told you that you have to retain control in every situation? Especially where men are concerned. Every confrontation between a man and a woman is a case of user and usee. You just have to make sure you are the one doing the using."

Addie stepped forward to lean against the wall beside the stairs. "Aren't you leaving love out of your equation?" she asked, her voice strangely soft.

"Love!" Delilah said in contempt. "Give me a break, Addie. I thought you had better sense. Don't you know that there is no such animal? What is popularly called love is just a wheelchair for emotional cripples . . . you feed my neurosis and I'll feed yours."

Glory shivered at the look on her friend's face as the blonde continued. "Men have known the truth of it for a long time and accept it for what it is. They know that if the sex is good, and if you don't actually throw up when you're with someone for longer than two hours, then that's enough. Don't look for more. And for heaven's sake, don't romanticize it. That's the way to suicide row."

Suddenly Delilah seemed to notice that there were other people around. Looking as close to embarrassment as Glory had ever seen her, the blonde stood and glanced quickly at her watch. "I'm late. See you two later." And without meeting their eyes, she ran down the stairs.

Glory stared at Delilah's retreating figure. A frown creased her brow. She had never seen her friend give in to emotion. It worried Glory knowing there was nothing any of them could do to help her.

"Sometimes she scares the hell out of me," Addie muttered, then moved to sit beside Glory. "Okay, let's have it. How come you're sitting out here?"

Glory shrugged, feeling a little hung over from all the emotional intensity she had encountered in one day. "I just needed time to think," she said.

"Something's wrong, Glory," Addie said, her voice suspicious. "What's he been doing to you? Why can't you just tell him it's none of his business and to forget he ever saw you?"

Glory frowned. It was strange that her worries about her father finding out had suddenly taken a backseat in her thoughts. Memory of the way she had felt when Alan kissed her filled every available space in her mind. She bit her lip. That proved that he was dangerous. He could make her forget everything.

"It's complicated, Addie," she said, smiling wryly when she realized how often she had said that lately.

Addie's eyes narrowed behind the thick glasses. "Is that man threatening you, Glory?"

Glory almost laughed. His mere presence threatened her, but not in the way Addie meant. As crazy as it sounded, when she was around Alan, she felt her whole future was at stake. And that frightened her.

"He scares me," she whispered aloud, then shook her head. "I'll work it out, Addie," she said, giving her roommate's hand a squeeze. "But thanks for caring."

Standing, Glory moved to the door of the apartment, unaware of the look on Addie's face as she followed her inside.

Eight

Alan leaned back on the couch, staring at the unfamiliar wall in the unfamiliar apartment. He glanced down at the woman pressed so closely against him. Her eyes were blue and welcoming. Nice eyes to go with all her other nice features. She was a warm, sensitive, intelligent woman . . . but she was the wrong woman.

He stood up abruptly. "I'm sorry . . . Tricia," he said, pulling her name up before it became embarrassing. "I'd better leave now."

"But you just got here." She appeared to be confused, and he could have kicked himself for being the cause of it.

"Yes, I know, but . . ." How to explain? he wondered. "I really wouldn't be good company for you. I've got . . . things on my mind."

The tall, slender woman stared at him in bewilderment. "You sound almost angry. Did I do something wrong?"

"No, of course not," he assured her. "If I sound angry, it has nothing to do with you."

Damn you, Glory, he thought as he drove away from Tricia's apartment. He cursed himself as well over the nice sane woman he had met at a party that night. But the truth was, the party and the woman had both been tools to keep him from calling Glory again.

In the two weeks since he had met her at the hospital, Alan had lost count of the times he had called her. He had even gone by her apartment once, only to meet with the obstacle of her roommates. She had said they were overprotective of her, and he had found that to be an understatement. The gold in Fort Knox didn't have such vigilant guards.

Damn stubborn woman, he thought in exasperation. It was time to write off Miss Gloria Wainwright. Alan had never been the type to chase after a woman . . . even if she did have eyes to start a war over.

When he walked into his apartment thirty minutes later, Alan had built his anger up to magnificent proportions. Flicking on the hall light, he shrugged out of his coat, dropping it in a chair as he headed toward the kitchen. He took a beer from the refrigerator, opened it, and took a long swallow.

He wouldn't give her another thought, he told himself firmly. He wouldn't call; he wouldn't dream of her.

Sitting at the small breakfast table, his head

dropped back, his eyes closed. Whom was he trying to kid? It would take brain surgery to cut Glory out of his thoughts. He could go to a hundred parties; he could make love to a thousand women; but he wouldn't stop thinking about Glory.

Reason had no place in the way he felt about Glory. Something fateful had begun the night he met her, something that had to be seen through to the end . . . whatever that end happened to be.

Tossing the empty bottle into the trash, he left the kitchen. Tomorrow he would go to the hospital. He would force a confrontation. And if nothing else, he would reassure her that he wouldn't tell her father about what she was really doing in Dallas.

He was on his way to the bedroom when the doorbell rang. He glanced at the watch on his wrist with a puzzled frown. It was after midnight; who would be stopping by at this time of night?

When he opened the door, his eyes widened in surprise. "What—" he began. Then there was only the sound of scuffling.

Glory opened the front door and headed up the stairs, her steps unusually slow. The strain of the past two weeks was beginning to take its toll. She was tired to death of worrying about her father while she kept up with her work. And Alan . . .

But she didn't want to think about Alan. She had acted like a fool, running away from him that night two weeks ago. Since she hadn't heard a word from him, there was no doubt in her mind that he would tell her father about her work. You didn't mess around with a man's ego without experiencing consequences.

She was running out of time. Her father would return to Austin in a couple of days. She had two choices. She could go to Alan, apologize for her behavior, and obtain his promise that he would keep her career a secret. Or she could tell her father everything.

Her head hurt from trying to come to a decision. Tension ached in her muscles. It was a nervous tension that had already spread to her roommates. They watched her constantly. Booger had had three birthdays in the last week alone. She wished she could turn the problem over to them, but there were some things she had to handle alone.

When she reached the apartment, she placed the key in the lock and wiggled it, but she couldn't summon enough strength for even a small kick. When it refused to open, she almost cried in frustration. She leaned against the door wearily.

It was time she faced the real problem. In her heart she knew that if she had explained the situation to him, Alan wouldn't go to her father with the truth. The problem was seeing him again.

"And one of these days," she muttered aloud, "when I'm not so dead tired, I'll have to think about why the thought of being with Alan terrifies the bejabbers out of me."

She shoved the door, and as though it had taken pity on her, it swung open. She walked across the dark living room, then paused when she saw a shape outlined on the couch. It was Jack.

She summoned up a small smile. Her room-mates had gone out partying tonight. This was probably as far into the apartment as he could get. Jack always gave his all to a party.

The afghan that should have been covering him had fallen to the floor. He was lying on his stomach, his electric blue bikini underwear standing out even in the darkness. Reaching down, she picked up the crocheted coverlet and spread it over him.

Without opening his eyes he grabbed her hand and mumbled, "S'awright, Glory. We fixed it."

"That's good," she said, her voice soft and soothing. "Go back to sleep and you can tell me all about it tomorrow."

"Tomorrow," he murmured, and went back to sleep.

What had they fixed? she wondered as she walked into her bedroom. They had probably come up with some wild scheme to spirit her out of the country so she could finish her internship in Zaire or somewhere equally impossible.

Without turning on the light she began to peel off her clothes. Enough moonlight filtered through the nylon curtains to light her way. The mirror caught her reflection, and for a moment Glory stopped to study it. Her body shone in the pale light of the moon, looking unnaturally white.

When was the last time she had lain in the sun? she wondered. Not that it really mattered. So many things had been shoved aside in the last four and a half years. She had used all her time, all her concentration, on becoming the best doctor she could be.

She ran a hand slowly down her body. Sometimes she almost forgot that she was a woman. That part of her, the woman part, had necessarily taken a backseat to her profession.

Closing her eyes, she realized that Alan made her remember that part. Was that why she had panicked when he suggested they see each other again? Was she afraid she wouldn't be able to handle more than one role at a time? Was it vaguely possible that her need to be a woman for him could overpower her need to be a doctor?

As though it were a clinical specimen, she examined her body, her small, firm breasts, the curve of her hips and thighs. She had been so determined that nothing would stop her from becoming a doctor. Had she given up too much in the process?

This was crazy, she thought, inhaling in exasperation. A month ago she had known exactly what she wanted. Her desire to be a doctor hadn't changed, but now she felt that it wasn't enough. Something was missing.

This biological garbage was a pain, she thought in frustration. Men never had a problem being professionals and men at the same time. She smiled wryly because she knew men weren't constantly being assaulted by revved-up hormones either.

She was a doctor; she knew what hormones could do. She should have guessed what her problem with Alan was. Her feminine urges had been constantly pushed aside, but rather than atrophying, as her father feared, they were building steadily, need piled upon need, just waiting around until someday they would burst in an awesome display.

And Glory was very much afraid that Alan was the man to make the dam burst. The nagging thought that he could easily become an obsession hounded her.

With a hand to the small of her back she stretched wearily. Glory had gone over the possibilities until her brain was numb. She had to get some sleep. When she was rested, she would tackle the problem.

She moved toward the bed, then stopped when she heard a muffled noise. This was all she needed, she thought. Glory didn't feel up to fighting for a place to sleep. She paid extra for this room, this bed; she was entitled to a place to lay her muddled head.

Sitting on the edge of the bed, she said softly, "Delilah. Dee, wake up. I need my bed." Glory reached out to shake her, then hastily she withdrew her hand. It wasn't Delilah.

A man was lying on her bed, his mouth taped with wide adhesive tape. She saw dark eyes shining in the moonlight.

Catching her breath sharply, she realized she knew those eyes. She would know them anywhere, even in the dark.

Nine

"Oh, my God. Oh, my God." Glory felt the words stick in her throat as she took in the adhesive tape on Alan's hands and feet. "They really did it. Oh, my God."

She stood, holding a hand to her mouth, her gaze never leaving him. His eyes shined in the darkness, insistent, demanding something of her. Thoughts flew chaotically about in her brain.

"I don't believe it," she whispered frantically. "How? How did they get you here?"

His eyes blazed and she realized it was frustration because he couldn't answer. Reaching out, she jerked on the wide tape covering his mouth.

"Sonofabitch!" Alan said, feeling half the skin on his upper lip go with the tape. "Did you have to pull it so damn hard?" His tongue sought the tender skin. "You've just depilated me."

She lifted a shaking hand to her head. "How—

what did they do? They didn't hurt you, did they? Please tell me they didn't knock you in the head or something."

Alan stared at her silently. He had been lying in the dark for hours, his anger building with each passing minute. But the minute he had seen her naked body, luminescent in the moonlight, all anger had disappeared. They could have nailed him to the bed, and he still would have been enchanted by the sight.

Standing beside the bed, Glory waited, her body tense. Words of rebuke had to come sooner or later. Suddenly she realized he wasn't speaking because he was staring at her breasts, her bare breasts. Swinging around quickly, she grabbed her robe from the hook on the wall and slipped into it.

Slowly she turned back to face him and the situation. Her eyes took on a hunted look as her gaze rested momentarily on the tape binding his hands and feet. "Oh, my God," she whispered again.

They had really done it this time. All the pranks, all the practical jokes, counted for nothing beside this escapade. The police could be looking for them right now. How on earth was she going to undo the damage her friends had done?

"I guess you know I can have every one of you arrested for this?" Alan said quietly.

His voice made her jump in startled reaction as he echoed aloud her very thoughts. He was a powerful man, she thought, biting her lip. He could cause trouble her friends would never be able to reverse. Without replying, she turned and rushed from the room.

Running to the couch, she began to shake Jack's shoulder urgently. "Jack . . . Jack, get up!" When he simply moaned and pulled the cover over his head, she jerked the afghan down and grabbed his hair, holding his face up level with hers. "Get up, you idiot!"

His eyes had a glazed look, but at last she was convinced he was awake. Turning away, she ran to Addie and Delilah's room. Flipping on the light switch, she moved to Addie's bed. "Addie, get up."

"What is it?" Addie said, her voice muffled by the pillow.

"Get up and bring Delilah with you . . . *now*," Glory added on her way out the door.

In Booger and Jack's room, Glory reached for the switch but flipped it to no avail. The bulb was burned out. She tripped twice on her way across the room and almost fell on top of Booger as she reached the bed. "Get up, Booger," she said, desperation growing in her voice.

The pillow hit her in the face as it came up to cover his head. She jerked it away, placed her mouth next to his ear and shouted, "Get up!"

"Don't yell," he moaned, holding his head as though in pain. "Just don't yell."

She drew in a deep breath. There was only one way to wake Booger up. "Emergency, Schlumburger," she said, her voice strict.

His eyes opened immediately. "What is it?"

"Come on," she called as she hurried back to the living room.

Jack, pulling on his jeans as he walked, followed her to the doorway of her bedroom. "You'd better have a good reason for this brutality, Glory," he said, his voice husky and irritated.

When she flipped on the light in her bedroom, he started to walk into the room, then stopped in his tracks, staring at the man on the bed. "Oh, hell," he whispered hoarsely. "Then it wasn't a dream."

As they stood staring in silence, the others joined them at the door. "What's going on?" Addie said.

Glory waved a hand toward the bed. For a moment she couldn't speak as she stared at them, her dearest friends, and they all stared at the man on the bed. Inhaling slowly, trying to calm her pounding heart, she said, "How could you do it?" She shook her head. "Do you even know what it is you've done, for *sweet heaven's sake*?"

Booger grabbed his head and moaned as her voice rose.

"Have a little pity," Addie said. "Booger doesn't feel well."

Gritting her teeth, Glory said, "Booger is going to feel a lot worse when you're all thrown in jail."

"I'm going to die," Booger moaned. "I'm really going to die."

Addie grabbed his arm and led him toward the kitchen. "You're not going to die. Let me see if I can find an Alka Seltzer."

Glory leaned against the doorjamb, closing her eyes in exasperation. They seemed to have no comprehension of what they had done. Surely she had told them what a powerful man Alan was. Did that mean nothing to them?

"Please," she said, her voice quiet and intense.

"Could someone explain to me how this could possibly have seemed like rational behavior."

"We did it for you," Jack said, sounding gruff and defensive.

"For me!" she said explosively, then exhaled slowly. When she spoke again, her voice was even but tight. "When—please tell me—when have I ever expressed a desire to be thrown into prison for the rest of my life?"

Jack shifted uncomfortably. Booger and Addie walked back from the kitchen, both looking unnaturally subdued. Delilah was the only one of the roommates who appeared unaffected by the situation.

"We didn't know what we were doing," Booger said, his voice contrite. "We went to the Cowhouse Saloon like we had planned and—"

"It's a fantastic place. Authentic Texas," Jack said, interrupting the explanation. "We taught Booger the Texas two-step and this really wild schottische." He chuckled, leaning closer. "You should have seen . . ." His voice faded away when he was pinned by the venom in Glory's eyes. "Sorry," he said contritely.

"Go ahead, Booger."

He rubbed his head. "After we had been there awhile, McIntire spotted us. You remember McIntire . . . pediatrics . . . red hair and a beer gut."

"I remember McIntire," she said, her voice tight with impatience.

He raised a hand to his head, rubbing his temples. "I can't remember too much of the next part,

"alluring"... "inspiring"...
"irresistible"...

Loveswept

America's most popular, most compelling romance novels.

Loveswept

Here, at last...love stories that really involve you! Fresh, finely crafted novels with story lines so believable you'll feel you're actually living them!

Read a Loveswept novel and you'll experience all the very real feelings of two people as they discover and build an involved relationship: laughing, crying, learning and loving. Characters you can relate to... exciting places to visit...unexpected plot twists...all in all, exciting romances that satisfy your mind and delight your heart.

And now you can be sure you'll never, ever miss a single Loveswept title by enrolling in our special reader's home delivery service. A service that will bring all four new Loveswept romances published every month into your home—and deliver them to you *before* they appear in the bookstores!

Examine 4 Loveswept Novels for

15 Days FREE!

To introduce you to this fabulous service, you'll get four brand-new Loveswept releases not yet in the bookstores. These four exciting new titles are yours to examine for 15 days without obligation to buy. Keep them if you wish for just $9.95 plus postage and handling and any applicable sales tax.

LOVESWEPT · 160
LOVESWEPT · 161
LOVESWEPT · 162
LOVESWEPT · 159
CHARLOTTE HUGHES
Too Many Husbands

SEND NO MONEY NOW.
RETURN THIS
POSTAGE-PAID CARD TODAY!

FREE TRIAL/HOME DELIVERY ORDER CARD

Loveswept
Bantam Books, P.O. Box 985, Hicksville, NY 11802

☐ Please send me four new romances for a 15-day FREE examination.
If I keep them, I will pay just $9.95 plus postage and handling and any
applicable sales tax and you will enter my name on your preferred cus-
tomer list to receive all four new Loveswept novels published each month
before they are released to the bookstores—always on the same 15-day
free examination basis.

20123

Name_____

Address_____

City_____

State_____ Zip_____

My Guarantee: I am never required to buy any shipment unless I wish. I
may preview each shipment for 15 days. If I don't want it, I simply return the
shipment within 15 days and owe nothing for it.

F123

BUSINESS REPLY MAIL

FIRST-CLASS MAIL   PERMIT NO. 2456   HICKSVILLE, NY

Postage will be paid by addressee

Loveswept

Bantam Books
P.O. Box 985
Hicksville, NY 11802

but I believe McIntire bought a round of drinks for us. Something called the Amarillo Annihilator, I think."

"It was the Waco Wrecker," Jack said.

"Yeah, that was it. Then everyone started buying his or her favorite drink for the table and . . . and after the Tequila Sunrises, I'm afraid everything is blank."

She stared at them in astonishment. "My God! It's a wonder you didn't poison yourselves." When Booger and Addie flinched, Glory bit her lip to keep from screaming at them. "So you were all in Lala Land. That still doesn't tell me why Alan Spencer is in this apartment, taped up like a medical student's nightmare, and lying on *my* bed!"

"I wasn't drunk."

Glory jerked around to stare at Delilah. It was the first time the blond woman had spoken. In her face there was no guilt, no contrition.

"I knew exactly what we were doing," Delilah continued firmly. Now Glory could see a hint of belligerence in her friend's face.

"Well, I wish to hell *I* did," she said, swinging around in frustration. "Someone please tell me how you got Alan here and what you did to him."

Four pairs of eyes turned to Delilah. The blonde shrugged. "In the cab on the way home we started talking about you. About how long it had been since we had seen you laugh, or even smile." She glanced at Glory, then nodded toward Alan. "Not since he showed up at the hospital. They got a little belligerent . . . I suppose the drinks contributed to that. But sober or not, we all wanted to do something to help."

She shrugged casually, as though she were discussing the price of tomatoes. "We decided to get Spencer here to the apartment and convince him to keep his mouth shut."

Glory closed her eyes. "And just like that you decided to kidnap a man," she said weakly.

Jack jerked his head around to stare at her, his expression horrified "But . . . no, you've got it all wrong. It's not kidnapping, at least, not exactly."

"What do you call it . . . exactly," Glory said, pinning each of them with her gaze. "The man is obviously here against his will. Or are you going to tell me this is some kind of bondage party and he's having fun."

"But he came here freely," Addie said. "It was only after we got him here that we taped him up."

"Freely?"

"Honestly, Glory," Jack said. "He was glad to come with us."

Her eyes narrowed. "You're leaving something out," she said, the words slow and suspicious. "There is something you're not telling me." When Jack and Addie shifted uncomfortably, Glory turned to Booger.

"I'm sorry, Glory," Booger said. "I can't remember a thing after the—"

"The Tequila Sunrises," she supplied for him. "Okay, Delilah," she said, turning to the blonde. "You remember. What are you not telling me?"

"Before we went to his apartment, we went to the hospital," Delilah said.

"The hospital?" she gasped. "My Lord, you didn't drug him. Please, for heaven's sake, say you didn't drug him."

"Glory!" Jack said. "What kind of people do you think we are?"

She laughed shortly. "I hate to repeat myself, but there is a man in my room who is bound hand and foot with adhesive tape. Do you really want me to tell you what kind of people I think you are?"

"Okay, okay," Jack said. "So maybe we're stupid, but we're not criminals. It isn't nearly as bad as you think. Addie remembered this movie she had seen the night before, where the bad guy was subdued by using ether."

"Ether?" she whispered, her voice incredulous. "You used ether on him?"

He shook his head. "No, the only thing we could get without get caught was a canister of . . . nitrous oxide," he finished reluctantly.

A yelp of startled laughter escaped her. "Laughing gas? You're honestly trying to tell me you kidnapped a man using *laughing gas?*"

They all relaxed visibly, as though relieved that she could laugh about it.

"You're crazy!" she shouted, ending their relief immediately. "Every one of you is stark, raving mad. Heaven help us, what did you do, jump out at him and slap the mask on his face?"

"It took all four of us to hold him down," Jack said, his eyes sparkling with something like pride, "but once we gave him some happy air, he was very cooperative."

"Brilliant, just brilliant," she said, shaking her

head in disbelief. Then she glanced at Delilah. "You were sober. Why didn't you stop them?"

"Stop them? It was my idea," Delilah said, her voice calm. She nodded over her shoulder toward the bed. "He was hurting you."

Delilah's voice sounded almost casual, but when Glory looked closer, she saw an anger that made her shiver. She hoped she never had the misfortune to cross Delilah.

"And I don't care if technically it is kidnapping," Delilah continued. "I'd do the same thing again tomorrow if I had to."

"But—" Glory stopped suddenly. After what they had gone through for her, how could she tell them that Alan wasn't the kind of threat they thought him to be. The danger was not in what Alan could do or say; the danger was in the way Glory felt about him.

Glory shook her head slowly. "Don't any of you understand?" she said, glancing at each of them in turn. "We can't keep him here forever, and the minute we let him go, he's going to have us all thrown in jail."

The five roommates turned as one to look into the bedroom at the man on the bed. He didn't move until he was sure he held their complete attention, then slowly his lips curved into a satisfied smile.

Alan lay silently watching as they filed slowly into the bedroom, each staring warily at him. They looked as though they were being pulled by invisible strings. Alan had moved his taped hands behind his head, making him appear the only relaxed one in the room.

"You people certainly get into strange situations," he said, shaking his head slightly. "It must be interesting to live here."

"What are we going to do?" Addie asked, ignoring Alan's remarks as she sat on a bench by the window.

Delilah moved to sit beside her. "I like Booger's original suggestion of locking him in the basement."

"I was teasing when I suggested that," Booger said as he and Glory sat at the foot of the bed on opposite sides. "I wish I could remember how we did this. It's very disconcerting to think I'm capable of violence."

"Actually," Alan said, his expression thoughtful, "you didn't contribute much to the caper . . . at least not wittingly. When you started leaning, one of the others leaned you in my direction. That was enough to pin me to the wall while they gassed me."

Glory moaned. It seemed so much worse when he said it like that. It sounded so premeditated, so inexcusably criminal. "What are we going to do?" she asked, echoing Addie's earlier question.

Jack jumped up to sit on the dresser. "We could always plead temporary insanity," he suggested wryly.

Glory shot a squelching look at him. "Insanity that just happened to strike four people at the same time?" she asked sarcastically.

"Glory's right," Alan said, his voice calm, almost pleasant. "They wouldn't buy it. We'll have to think of something else."

Addie bit her thumbnail. "If we let him go, he'll go straight to the police," she said to the room at large.

"Did anyone see the *Invasion of the Body Snatchers*?" Alan asked conversationally.

"But then, on the other hand," Addie continued, "we can't keep him here forever. Not even if we put him in the basement with the peach preserves."

"Everyone started changing personalities, but it was because aliens had taken over their bodies—" Alan said.

Booger glanced at each of them in turn. "I think the only thing we can do is to admit what we've done and throw ourselves on the mercy of the court. Surely they can look at our backgrounds and see that we're not criminals."

"So what you should do," Alan continued, "is start by telling the police about these giant pods."

Delilah stood and walked close to the bed, staring at Alan venomously. "All this is your fault, but we're the ones who will get in trouble for it."

He smiled slowly. "You've certainly got a problem, haven't you?"

"We can't go to the police," Jack said, ignoring Delilah's outburst. "Remember last Halloween?"

"But that didn't go on our record," Addie said. "Those people got over being mad as soon as they got their ostrich back."

"That's not the point," Glory said. "Jack's right. The police will remember us. How often do they get a bird of that size running around the police station?"

"A jailbird?" Alan said, intrigued by the disjointed pieces of the story.

He wasn't used to being ignored so completely, but that didn't dim his enjoyment of the scene. The group moved into the other room and as Alan listened to the chagrin and even fear in their voices, all his indignation and anger disappeared. While not exactly a bunch of kids, they were still very young. And if that fact had not swayed him, their protective attitude toward Glory would have.

"Wait a minute," Addie said, taking off her glasses to rub the bridge of her nose. "Isn't there some kind of law that says a husband can't testify against his wife?"

Glory brought a hand to her forehead, then glanced in disbelief at Addie. "So what am I supposed to do?" she asked dryly. "Marry him to keep us all out of jail? It would take more than laughing gas to accomplish that. I can't believe you even said that, Addie."

"Okay, okay. I'm just getting desperate." She glanced at Booger. "Come on, Booger. You're the brains of this outfit. Think of something."

Booger rubbed his temples. "I can't think. That Waco Wrecker dissolved my brain. I can hear it sloshing around in there . . . I think if I lean over, it'll all come out my ears." He glanced around the room warily. "Besides, I'm very much afraid there isn't a solution to this. At least not one that we'll be able to live with."

"Oh, I don't know," Alan shouted to them. "I think we should give Addie's suggestion more consideration."

Glory turned to look at him for the first time since entering the other room. She stared at the suppressed laughter in his eyes and smiled tentatively. "Alan," she said softly as she walked back into her bedroom, "you can see they meant no harm. They didn't know what they were doing."

"I did," Delilah said firmly.

"Delilah, be quiet." Glory turned back to Alan. "Couldn't you just consider it a joke that went wrong and let it go at that?"

The laughter faded from his eyes as he studied her earnest expression. "You can call it anything you want to," he said, his words slow and soft. "Legally your peculiar friends kidnapped me, and if nothing else, you are an accessory after the fact."

Jack moaned and dropped his head to his hands. "My parents will kill me if they hear about this. I might as well go to South America right now and get it over with. I can just see myself delivering babies in some village hospital while flies buzz around the instruments and chickens run in and out of the delivery room."

"Parents . . . and the hospital," Addie groaned, her eyes opening wide. "Do you realize what will happen when the hospital board finds out we've been arrested?"

"I've been thinking of growing a beard anyway," Booger said, his voice melancholy.

Jack snorted. "You'd look like Burl Ives, Jr. And anyway, your father is a bigshot doctor; he can pull strings for you. My father is a retired mailman."

"Why didn't one of you think of this before you kidnapped me?" Alan asked, trying with difficulty to keep from laughing. "Didn't anyone mention it was against the law?"

Addie jumped up and walked over to him. "This isn't funny. And anyway, we wouldn't have done it if you hadn't threatened Glory."

His eyes narrowed, and slowly he turned to look at Glory. "Did I threaten you, Glory?"

Color suffused her face. She closed her eyes briefly, then softly she said, "No."

Suddenly everyone was back in Glory's room with their eyes on her. Alan watched her closely, wondering what was going on in her mind at that moment.

"But you said he scared you," Addie said, her expression confused. "I thought . . . we all thought that he had threatened to tell your father if you didn't . . ." Her voice faded into a helpless shrug.

"If she didn't what?" Alan asked, his eyes never leaving Glory's face.

Addie waved a hand exasperatedly. "How should we know? She's been looking all withdrawn and antsy ever since you showed up at the hospital." She glanced at Glory. "And she did say you scared her."

"Did you, Glory?" he said softly. "Now, I wonder why you would say a thing like that."

She met his eyes for a moment, not long enough for him to find any answers, but long enough to see that the conversation made her extremely uncomfortable.

"None of this makes any difference," Glory said, trying to keep her voice calm. She figured one of them should stay sane. "For whatever reason, the deed is done. And we've still got to figure a way out of this mess." Squaring her shoulders, she glanced at Alan. "You're the one in control here. What can we do to appease your . . . your sense of outrage?"

"My *righteous* outrage," he corrected her.

"Very well, your righteous outrage," she conceded reluctantly. "Surely we don't have to go to jail to make up for your inconvenience?"

"I'm in control, you say," he said thoughtfully. "That's a curious position for a man who is bound hand and foot to be in. I'll have to think about it."

"Come on, Alan," she said in exasperation. "I know you feel you've been wronged and are enjoying prolonging our agony, but could you stifle your peculiar sense of humor long enough to resolve this thing?"

The laughter in his eyes faded. "Get them out and we'll talk," he said, his voice devoid of emotion. No more games. It was time to get on with it.

Reaction in the room was instant. Glory's roommates all spoke at the same time.

"Where do you get off?"

"No!"

"You don't have to take orders from him."

"Glory," Booger said, a rarely seen frown changing his bland features, "we got you into this and we'll get you out. We just need time to come up with something."

Glory shook her head. She knew the only way they could settle this was through Alan. "It won't hurt to talk to him," she said. "You'll all be in the living room; what could possibly happen to me?"

They stared at her for a moment, indecision

etched in four very different faces. Then Booger stood and moved toward the door. The others slowly followed him out.

Glory closed the door behind them, then turned warily back to Alan. She was more nervous than she had ever been, but she refused to let him see that. "Okay, we're alone," she said quietly. "What can we do to clear this up?"

He studied her face. "You're very calm. It's a change from your screwball roommates."

"Let's leave my friends out of this," she said tightly.

"That might be difficult to do," he said with a faint smile. "They are the ones who started all this."

"They thought they were protecting me."

He watched her carefully. "I've been lying here listening to you all, trying to make sense of this, but I can't. I wanted to see you again. A simple no would have been sufficient. Why did you run away then refuse to take my phone calls?"

Glory glanced away from him to stare at the crack in the ceiling. She hadn't known about the calls. Her roommates had certainly been busy little darlings. The silence became obvious, and she knew he was waiting for an answer, but she didn't have one to give him. She had asked herself the same question time after time to no avail.

"Addie said you were afraid of me," he asked softly. "Why? What have I ever done to make you afraid of me?"

She dropped her eyes to his, trying to form an answer. Several lies occurred to her, but she merely shook her head and glanced back at the ceiling.

"Come sit down, Glory," he said, his voice becoming husky against his will. As she sat on the bed, several feet from him, she looked vulnerable. And she looked angry that it should be so.

"You weren't afraid I would do you physical harm, were you?" he asked.

Inhaling slowly, she said, "No."

"Then what was it?"

She shivered slightly, then her back straightened, and she turned to look at him. "None of that matters. I thought you wanted to talk about this situation . . . about what we can do . . . what I can do to keep my friends out of jail."

He stared at her for a moment, then smiled wistfully. "I'm sorry. It's a little hard to think. My lips hurt. You took most of the skin off with that tape."

Glory stared at him, feeling confused at the change of subject. Then she saw the expectant look in his eyes and understood. He wanted her to apologize. She inhaled slowly. "In all the confusion, it escaped my mind, but I do most sincerely apologize for what we've put you through . . . the nitrous oxide, the tape. And I'm sorry I hurt you."

There, she thought, it was done. He was a reasonable man. Surely now he would let it all drop.

One thick brow rose in inquiry. "That's it?" he asked in disbelief. "I tell you my lips hurt and you give me a stiff, half-hearted apology to make it better."

"Make it better?" she said, a confused frown settling on her features. Suddenly her eyes opened wide. "Make it better?" she repeated. He still wanted to play games, and there was not a damn thing she could do about it. He held all the cards.

Moving closer, she leaned toward him. His eyes stayed open, studying her features intently. She stopped and felt drawn into the depths of his brown eyes. Then hurriedly she brushed her lips against his.

"Now," she briskly, "you've effectively demonstrated your power. I have humbled myself because I know we're in the wrong and I want to make up for that. Will you promise not to go to the police?"

Frowning, he looked at her. "You call that a kiss?" he asked skeptically. "That might work on a little scratch; this is a major injury."

Glory felt fury explode inside her. Before she could think, she reached out and clasped his face roughly with both her hands as she leaned forward.

Alan saw anger in the rigid line of her spine and the blue blaze of her eyes, but when she touched him, he drew in a sharp breath and nothing mattered but the feel of her mouth on his. Slipping his bound hands over her head, he pulled her closer, moving his body into hers.

He had waited so long to be this close to her, to have the full length of her body pressed against his. He had dreamed of it, visualized it, but his imagination hadn't come anywhere near the reality.

It felt so damn right. He tasted her lips as he felt the anger in her drain away. His tongue sought the intimacy he craved. He wanted to be inside her.

Every muscle in his body was demanding that he become a part of her.

When he felt her tongue move slightly against his, a muffled sound of triumph came from deep in his throat. He had felt desire for women often in the past, but nothing so all-consuming, nothing that wiped out every other thought, every other emotion. His body strained toward her softness, the hard tension building in him immeasurably. If it was this strong when he simply kissed her, what would it be like when they made love?

The thought of making love to her sent an electric shock through him, and suddenly Alan was afraid. He had never felt anything like this. It was all happening too fast. He needed time to think.

Pulling back, he stared into blue eyes that echoed the chaos in his own. She didn't move away, but simply stared back, her eyes moving from his mouth to trace the lines of his face. Her hair fell across her face, her lips swollen and moist from the kiss.

Alan's smile was unsteady. "I've never really gotten into bondage, but"—he swallowed heavily—"I think I could get used to it."

Without taking her eyes from his face, she reached behind her neck to pull his hands over her head. "It wasn't tight," she murmured when his hands were free of the tape. "You could have taken it off with your teeth."

"I could have," he confirmed softly. He reached out to touch her face. He had simply intended to brush the hair from her cheek, but when he touched her face, his fingers acted on their own, cupping her jaw, urging her close again.

Her eyelids drooped, giving her a sensual, exciting look. Suddenly she blinked as though coming out of a deep sleep and pulled away from him. She stood up.

"Is that all?" she asked, her voice husky. Her breasts rose and fell rapidly, as though she had been running. "Can I tell my friends that everything's been taken care of?"

Reaching down, he pulled the tape from his ankles. A frown put deep grooves in his strong face as he swung around to sit on the side of the bed and stare at her intently. She had looked fragile the first night they met. Now she looked as though a slight gust of wind would blow her away. There were dark circles under her eyes, and her cheeks were hollow. What in hell had she been doing to herself?

"What are you doing coming in at four in the morning?" he asked gruffly, annoyed that he should be so deeply concerned for her welfare.

She looked puzzled by the question and shook her head as though to clear it. "I was working," she said reluctantly. "What does that have to do with anything?"

He stood, shoving his hands into his pockets as he stared at her. "Why do you have to work such ridiculous hours?"

"Alan," she said in exasperation, "forget about my job. Haven't you carried the joke far enough? Will you give me your word that you won't press charges?"

He studied her face, frowning, then he turned away and walked to the window. The room was silent for quite a while, then he turned around and slowly shook his head. "No, I'm sorry. I can't do that."

"But—"

"There is one more thing I want you to do, then I'll give my word."

She looked at him suspiciously. "What?"

"I want you to come away with me for a week."

For a moment Glory didn't speak; she couldn't. It was too much. Coming on top of the kiss that had nearly destroyed her, it was too much to take. "What are you talking about?" she asked hoarsely.

"I think I made myself clear," he said, his tone cool, utterly unemotional. "I want you to come away with me. In exchange, your friends will keep their records clean."

"That's blackmail," she said, then laughed tightly. "I certainly made a mistake reading your character. I thought you were too civilized to use force."

"Force?" he said, walking toward her. His quiet voice and casual steps couldn't disguise his iron strength. "Lady, you don't know what you're talking about. Force is being assaulted. Force is being taped up, hand and foot, by four slightly cracked medics. I know about force. You, on the other hand, are free to choose what you want to do. You can tell me to go to hell, and let your friends rot in jail. Or you can spend a week with me in San Padre . . . either way it's your choice."

Glory closed her eyes against the bluntness of

his words. She had to look at this logically. He wanted revenge, retribution for a wrong committed against him. Glory could accept that; she would probably have done something similar if their situations were reversed.

How's that for logic? she thought wryly.

Then suddenly, like a bolt of lightning, Glory knew what was wrong—she wanted to go with him! She wanted to throw caution to the wind and go away with a man she barely knew. In fact, she wanted it very much, and that was why she couldn't do it.

At that moment voices filtered in from the living room, interrupting her thoughts. Biting her lip, Glory glanced toward the door. She had forgotten her friends. They had tried to protect her. She owed them something for that.

She had never had an alternative. Almost resenting the excitement that suddenly shook her as she reached her decision, she said, "I'll go."

Ten

San Padre, Texas

Glory opened her eyes to bright sunlight. For a few moments she lay somewhere between sleep and waking, aware, vaguely at first, then with a sharpening intensity, of a sense of well-being and expectation, a feeling reminiscent of Christmas mornings in childhood.

She was in an unfamiliar but beautiful room, lying on an unfamiliar but wonderfully soft bed. Somewhere outside there were gulls, and for a while she simply lay still, listening to their raucous talk.

Suddenly she remembered Alan, and immediately the blood in her veins quickened with his memory. Then, as though the thought had somehow materialized, the door opened, and he walked into the room.

Glancing at the loaded tray he carried, she said, "What's that?"

"Breakfast," he said simply. "It's time for lunch, but on the chance you might be one of those people who have to have their meals in order, I brought breakfast."

Glory realized she was starving. Glancing under the covers, she was pleased to find her body covered by her blue cotton nightshirt. Sitting up eagerly, she allowed him to arrange the tray across her lap.

"I take my meals any way I can get them, thank you, usually on the run," she said, brushing the tumbled hair from her face as she stared at the full tray. It was a meal fit for a king . . . or an Olympic boxer.

She glanced up, lifting one arched brow quizzically. "This is revenge?" She picked up a piece of buttered toast. "Remind me to offend you more often in the future," she said through a mouthful.

Sitting on the edge of the bed, he laughed, his dark eyes sparkling. "I'm trying to lull you into a false sense of security. Drink your milk."

"It's working," she said, picking up the glass to obey. After she had almost drained the glass, she inhaled deeply. "I feel great. I didn't realize I was so tired. This is the first time in four and a half years that I've stopped working. Even in med school I spent my weekends and vacation at a free clinic in south Dallas." She grinned broadly. "It's like I finally gave my body permission to collapse."

He smiled, his eyes never leaving her face. "Eat your eggs," he murmured.

"Why do you keep staring?" She took a healthy bite of the scrambled eggs. "I know I look a mess, but it's rude to remind me of that, even silently."

She felt at a disadvantage. He was dressed and had obviously been up for quite a while. The sleeves of the green cotton shirt he wore with his jeans were rolled up to reveal strong, tanned forearms.

"You look delightfully disheveled," he said, smiling as he ran his gaze over the black hair tumbling about her shoulders. He reached out to push the errant curl from her forehead. "If I'm staring, it's because I expected indignation from you at the very least."

"I'm indignant," she assured him, then swallowed all of her orange juice in one greedy gulp. "In fact, I'm mad as hell. I've just never felt very comfortable with hysterics, and I haven't got the face for sulking." She stopped eating long enough to give him a demonstration, nodding in chagrin when he laughed. "You see what I mean. Lord, I'm hungry. It seems like days since I've eaten."

She glanced up. "I don't usually eat this much . . . or sleep so long. Last night is a gray blur. I barely remember the flight here."

"You slept through most of it," he said. "The flight attendant thought you were drunk because you kept nodding into your fruit cup."

"How embarrassing for you," she said, her grin minimizing the sympathetic tone as she took the slice of bacon he held out to her. "I can recall vague bits of the flight, but for the life of me, I can't remember getting here." She waved the bacon like a wand, indicating the bedroom. "Or getting dressed for bed." She shrugged. "I'm glad I had sense enough to put on a nightshirt. I don't usually—"

Finding herself on too intimate territory, she broke off and accepted a piece of toast he had spread carefully with strawberry jam.

"Yes," he said softly, "I remember what you usually wear to bed. I don't think I'll ever forget." He smiled when her cheeks turned pink, staring as though the sight fascinated him. Then he met her gaze. "As a matter of fact, you were out too soundly to undress yourself last night. I did it for you. And I will never again doubt my self-control, Glory. You have a beautiful body."

Leaning forward, he brushed a kiss across her lips. "Strawberry is my favorite," he murmured, then stood up abruptly. "Finish your breakfast and meet me on the beach. You need some sunshine."

With her lips slightly parted, she sat for a moment in a warm daze. Then, swallowing heavily, she turned back to her breakfast. She managed two more hasty bites before sliding the tray aside.

She jumped from the bed and hurried to the closet. Instead of finding her unpacked suitcase, she discovered her clothes hanging neatly. Her underwear were in a small chest of drawers.

"Funny how one can become resigned to one's fate," she murmured to herself as she pulled a bright yellow sweatshirt over her head.

Resigned? she thought with a skeptical grin as she caught sight of her glowing face in the mirror. Okay, she conceded with reluctant honesty, the truth was that sometimes one positively welcomed one's fate.

The second she had agreed to come away with him, Glory had felt the tension uncoil inside her. She had fought thinking of him, had seen him as a threat, but when matters were taken out of her hands, she relaxed. The decision had not been of her making. She hadn't chosen this course. Therefore she was free to enjoy being with Alan.

It was all very simple. Their time together was not a beginning, it was an end. Glory was caught up in tit for tat. These were terms she had no trouble dealing with, even relishing, if the truth were known.

She smiled slightly. Someday she might even be able to tell her roommates about it. She hadn't actually lied to them when she left. She had explained that she needed to get away for a while and had arranged a leave of absence with the hospital. It wasn't Glory's fault that they assumed she was with her father in Austin, she thought righteously as she stepped into comfortable worn jeans.

After running a brush through her tangled hair, she pulled it up into a ponytail, then picked up the breakfast tray to return it to the kitchen.

Outside the bedroom door a hall ran the length of the house. Heading for the open end, she took in the watercolors decorating the white walls, each detail giving one more clue to Alan's character.

She glanced around with avid interest as she passed through the large open living area on her way to the kitchen. It was bright and modern, not a somber stroke in sight. One end of the room was dominated by a white stone fireplace, and running the length of the room was a glass wall, the white drapes pulled back to allow a wide view of the ocean. A beautiful frame for a beautiful picture.

In the kitchen she placed the breakfast tray on the cobalt-blue-tiled counter, then walked to the sliding glass doors. Through the glass she saw the same pristine stretch of beach she had seen from the living room. Pale pink sand, blue-green ocean, and bright azure sky.

For a moment she thought the beach was deserted, then to the left she picked out Alan's tall figure at the water's edge, his eyes shaded with one hand as he watched the sea gulls swoop and dive in joyous flight.

Sliding the door open, she stepped out onto a wooden deck, immediately raising her face to the sun. Eager enthusiasm hastened her steps as she crossed the deck, then skipped down the stairs to the sand. She was laughing for no discernible reason when she reached him.

"Hi," she said, inhaling deeply of the salt air as she stood beside him.

Glancing down at her, Alan couldn't help smiling. There was something totally endearing about her face, now bare of makeup. He had heard her running across the sand toward him and had felt the rhythm of his pulse change in anticipation, felt excitement race through his bloodstream.

But now was not the time to explore what he was feeling, he told himself firmly. She needed rest, food, and a complete absence of tension.

Taking her hand, he began to walk parallel to the

water's edge, letting the warmth of her presence blend with the warmth of the sun. He had visited his beach house frequently in the last two years, but never until today had he felt it was a home.

After a few moments of comfortable silence Glory said, "It feels strange not having to think about anything. I guess it's going to take a little practice." She glanced around. "Addie would love this place. She's a California beach freak . . . a little out of step in Dallas."

"Miss your roommates already?" he asked, making his voice casual to disguise a twinge of unreasonable jealousy.

She smiled. "They've been my family for a long time. In the beginning, when I looked at my funds and realized money would be tight, I thought of myself as being alone in this terrifically noble struggle." Her gurgle of laughter made fun of that younger Glory. "I was very dramatic at that age. Ethically I could have paid for food and clothes and rent with the allowance Daddy gives me, but I wanted to show him that I could make it on my own. When I found the apartment, I figured I could swing it if I had two roommates to share the cost, so Addie and Jane joined me. Jane left after about nine months, and Booger took her place."

Shading her eyes, she looked up at the sea gulls, then glanced back to Alan to continue. "It wasn't long after that that Delilah showed up and needed a place. Addie didn't mind sharing her room, so Dee moved in. Then Jack started hanging around . . . and hanging around. He would sleep three nights out of four on the sofa. Gradually, very sneakily, more and more of his things began to turn up in the apartment. Before we knew what had happened, he was one of the roommates." She smiled. "They are dear, dear people."

"They are weird, weird people," he muttered, then laughed at her pretended umbrage. "You have to admit you are an odd assortment."

"Maybe," she conceded, "but somehow we mesh. We all have different strengths. When one of us sags, the others hold him up." She glanced down at the sand beneath their feet. "Sometimes . . . sometimes when I think of us all splitting up to go our different ways, it makes me incredibly sad."

He thought of friends he had made in college. "It won't be the same, I agree," he said, his voice sympathetic. "But there are telephones, and the mail is pretty reliable. You don't have to let go completely."

"I know. And I know we'll always be friends. I guess it's more a little trepidation regarding the future and change." She shrugged. "On the one hand, I can't wait to start a practice of my own, but on the other, I know that this particular special time will never be duplicated."

He stared for a moment at the wistful twist of her soft lips. "Tell me about them, these weird friends of yours. What is it about each one that draws you?" When she threw him a doubtful glance, he said, "No, you're right. I'm not that interested in the roommates as separate individuals, but I'd like to know why they are special to *you*. Tell me about Booger . . . Lord, what a name."

She laughed. "He likes it better than Arnold." She stopped walking to look up at the sky. "Booger never does the expected. He introduced himself to me because he hoped I was related to Loudon Wainwright III. You see, Booger's president of the local fan club."

"Loudon who?"

"He's a composer-singer, but that's just what I mean. Booger never does the expected." She smiled. "What can I say about him? He's the warmest, most caring person I know. He's a genius, but never wears his IQ on his forehead. He is—not complacent," she said, shaking her head, "I guess tolerant is the word I'm looking for—of all human behavior because he says it's natural, and intriguing as hell to observe."

Bending down to pick up a shell, he said, "And Addie?"

"Oh, Addie is all gruff stuff on the outside, but on the inside she's warm Malt-o-meal on a cold morning. She's belligerently loyal to anyone she considers a friend." She laughed. "Addie is a firm believer in tough love."

He listened to the warmth in her voice. Then, studying her expression closely, he said quietly, "Jack?"

He saw her smile widen. "Mr. Moto? He should be here to tell you about himself. It's one of his favorite things. Jack thinks that the worst natural disaster imaginable is a world without him in it. Vanity's name is not woman; it's Jack. But he's also intelligent, quick-witted, and very, very loving to his friends."

After a moment of silence Alan said, "He's very attractive."

She glanced at him from the corner of her eye. "And you're wondering if I'm attracted?" she asked, smiling. "No way. At least not the way you mean. To get romantically involved with Jack would be fatal. I would then cease to be a friend. You see, Jack puts people in compartments. To us, his friends, he's loyal and true. But he doesn't see the women he dates as friends. They are a necessary, fun part of life. Someday he's going to find a woman who will make him like and respect her as well as desire her, and then his whole world will go topsy-turvy. But not me."

The brilliance of his smile made Glory stare and wonder why he was so pleased. After a moment he said, "Delilah?"

Shaking her head to bring her mind back to reality, she said, "Delilah? She's beautiful, intelligent, sexy, and would fight an army for anyone who has earned her friendship. Other than that I can't tell you much. She's a mystery. She let slip once that she had been on her own since she was fourteen, but that's all I know about her past. From all appearances she has no past, no family, no intimate friends except the roommates." She shrugged. "In a way she's a female Jack. She doesn't let any of the men she dates touch her emotionally. She has allowed the roommates to penetrate her wall just a little. But none of us really knows Delilah. She tries to convince everyone that she wanted to be a doctor for the money . . . and for a while I believed her and accepted it." She smiled. "Then I saw her work. She's not only a brilliant, intuitive healer, she's a genuinely caring person with her patients."

Catching her arm, he pulled her down to sit on the sand beside him. "Now comes the roommate who interests me the most. Tell me about Glory."

"Ah, Glory," she said, her expression serious as she nodded. "Glory is wonderful—"

"And warm and witty and wise," he said softly, smiling at her skeptical glance. "In fact, all that is bright and true. I agree wholeheartedly, but I want to know what motivates her. What's important to Glory? What were you like as a little girl in pigtails?"

Wrapping her arms around her knees, she rested her chin on them and gazed out across the water. "I didn't have pigtails, but I could have had them if I wanted them. Daddy would have bought them for me. I had everything else. In fact, I had a storybook childhood. No traumas, no dark spots. But—" She turned her head to look at him. "Do you have brothers or sisters?"

"Both. Two sisters and a brother."

She smiled. "I bet you're the oldest."

He frowned. "As a matter of fact, I am, but I don't think I like the fact that you guessed. It means you recognize something in me from Psychology 101—Behavior and Attitudes of the Firstborn Sibling, or some such nonsense." When she merely laughed, he said, "What does all that have to do with your childhood?"

"I was an only child," she said. "Although my parents treated me like a princess out of a fairy tale, I don't think any only child can escape feeling lonely sometimes. When I got older, it was an added burden because, with all their affection, all their concentration turned on me, every sin, every small accomplishment, was magnified." She dipped her head slightly. "When Mama died, I was fourteen. I was devastated, but Daddy was lost. I didn't know what to do to help him, but I tried. We were drawn even closer together."

"That's good, surely?"

She nodded. "Yes, but it meant he had even more time and motive to concentrate on me. My mother was an extremely fragile person—physically, not mentally. Since I'm very like her in appearance, Daddy has always assumed I am too. After she died, he tried to wrap me in gauze." She bent to draw a finger through the sand. "And more often than not, I let him. I thought he needed to think about me to keep his mind off Mama. He had lost two people he loved—"

"Two?"

She shifted her position slightly. "His younger brother died when I was seventeen," she said softly. "Daddy was twelve years older than Uncle Peter, and when their parents died, Daddy more or less raised him."

"Then he died and your father was even more watchful of you than before," Alan said, his voice understanding.

She nodded, then turned to meet his gaze. "I don't want to give you the wrong impression. I've been very lucky, very privileged all my life. Anything I wanted Daddy would get for me."

"Except the thing you wanted most—a career in

medicine. You had to get that for yourself," he said. "So that's why you kept it secret from him. He's afraid it's too tough a career for you." He paused for a moment. "I still think if you would let your father in on what's happening in your life, he would understand. Fathers have an annoying habit of doing that. You've made it through med school on your own. No fragile piece of porcelain could have."

She was silent for quite a while, staring down at the sand. "What I've told you is only part of it. There are . . . other reasons I can't tell him." She inhaled, turning her head to smile up at him. "So now you know all about Glory. Turnabout's fair play. Do you make a habit of extortion?"

"Extortion?" he asked, a solitary brow rising in haughty inquiry.

"Have you forgotten already? After all, it's the only reason I'm here," she said. Glory frowned suddenly, realizing that although her words were accusing, the tone was alarmingly carefree.

His dark gaze drifted over her thoughtful face. "Is it?" he asked softly.

Swallowing with difficulty, she stared at the intense expression on his face. It was incredible, the amount of electricity that would flow between them at times. Before she could form an answer to his question, she heard a shout a short distance away and turned with relief toward the noise.

A small, chubby little boy and a scruffy gray dog ran together down the beach. The boy waved as he passed, unaware or unconcerned that he was trespassing. A few yards down the beach dog got tangled up with boy and they took a nosedive. Both were up instantly, never missing a beat in the joyful run. It was only when an adult voice reached the boy from what was obviously the direction of home that he turned and left the beach once more to the sole possession of Alan and Glory.

Glory laughed, then stopped suddenly when she found his eyes trained on her face.

"You didn't answer my question," he said, his voice husky. "Is that the only reason you're here?"

She didn't know how to answer him. It was something she avoided thinking about. It was easier to say she was with him because she had no choice.

But this time it was Alan himself who prevented her from answering. Lowering his head, he brushed his lips across hers. If he had intended the kiss to be a friendly gesture, it went sadly awry. When their lips met, conscious thought was forgotten and sensation took over.

Glory's eyes drifted shut as she let the kiss fill her. She felt something wonderful, something compelling enter her bloodstream. This was what she had been waiting for. When she involuntarily moved closer, she felt him draw in a deep breath in reaction.

Now it would come, she thought. The thing that had been in the back of her mind since that first meeting. Now he would lead her into the house, to his bedroom, and they would make love. She would be able to ride the sensation to the end.

He pulled back, one hand on her cheek as he

stared at her. Surely he recognized the desire in her eyes, Glory thought feverishly.

After an endless moment he stood, pulling her up after him, and they began to walk again, his arm around her waist. But they didn't walk toward the house. They simply walked slowly along the beach.

Frowning, Glory stole a glance at his face. It wasn't exactly solemn, more contemplative, but she felt shut out. She bit her lip, unable to figure out what had happened. Why had he stopped? There was no way she could have mistaken the urgency in the kiss.

Then her eyes brightened. Alan was probably a night person, she thought in relief. If she was right, then tonight after dinner would be the time.

Having settled the matter to her satisfaction, Glory gave herself up to enjoying the day. Later in the afternoon, at her request, they visited the Padre Island National Seashore, crossing the Laguna Madre on the long causeway. The protected seashore was a lovely eighty miles of beach and dunes, little tufts of grass growing on piles of pale pink sand.

Leaving the car, they walked hand in hand while birds of unnumbered variety followed them from above.

"I remember the first time we came here," Alan said. "Joey was four, I was ten."

"Joey?"

"My brother. My two sisters, Jenny and Sara are normal human beings, but Joey is something else," Alan said with obvious affection. "You should meet him, Glory. He would fit right in with your weird friends. Being the youngest, he rebelled very early against, 'Why can't you be more like your brother and sisters,' and has spent his life in a quest for the outrageous. I must have pulled him out of the water a dozen times that day."

"Where is he now?" she asked, stooping to pick up a curly shell.

"In California, for the moment, making a movie that protests protest movies."

"That sounds . . . original," she said doubtfully.

He laughed. "Oh, he's that all right. He tried to talk me into appearing in it."

"And you turned him down?" she asked, her tone aghast, her eyes sparkling with fun.

He glanced at her with a smile. "Have you ever heard of a credibility level?"

She shook her head. "Sounds ominous. Does it have anything to do with blood sugar?"

"It has to do with my facing a room full of businessmen without knowing which of them might have seen me in what amounts in soft core pornography. My credibility level would drop to zero if I let myself be talked into appearing in one of Joey's films."

"Ah, the problems of the international executive," she said sympathetically, her lip quivering.

"How long has it been since you've been spanked," he said, his dark eyes narrowing.

She grabbed his hand, laughing outright. "Don't go kinky on me," she said. "Come on. Let's go see what those birds are harassing."

The fact that the birds were harassing a peanut

butter and jelly sandwich brought civilization a little closer to them but couldn't diminish Glory's enjoyment of the afternoon. By the time they headed back to San Padre, dusk was spreading its shadows over the land.

With each passing minute Glory felt an excitement build inside her at the thought of what the evening would bring. But as they prepared dinner together, she wondered if she had been mistaken in believing he would make his move that night. There was nothing of the lover in his actions. He kidded her like a younger sister. And all through the meal he seemed more concerned with making her clean her plate than with getting her into his bed.

"That's enough," she protested when he tried to give her the last of the huge, fresh shrimp on the platter. Pushing away from the table, she added, "I can't eat another bite, and I swear if you try to make me, I'll explode." She laughed. "And what a disgusting picture that would make—little bits of Glory all over the walls."

"Little bits of glory," he repeated slowly. "I like the sound of that. Every time I kiss you it's a little bit of glory."

Her gaze was soft as she stared at him. "That's nice," she said. "You've turned poetic suddenly." She lowered herself to the rug in front of the fire. "It makes a welcome change from the dictator who was intent on stuffing me like a Christmas turkey. What are you trying to do, fatten me up for the kill? I feel like poor Hansel."

"You don't look a bit like him," he said, sitting

beside her on the rug. "Stop complaining. You could use at least ten pounds. I was beginning to think you would blow away along with the leaves on the trees."

She stared at him, her eyes wide with horror. "You're not going to try to put ten pounds on me while we're here?" she gasped.

"No," he said, laughing. "Although after what you told me today, I hesitate to say it, but I just want you to stop looking so fragile."

She raised one brow in inquiry. "Are you afraid I'll break when you try to collect what's owed you?" Reaching out, she patted his hand where it rested on his raised knee. "Poor thing, what an uncomfortable position to be in."

He stared at her for a moment, his eyes narrowing. "Glory," he said softly. "Lean closer to me, darling."

She bit her lip to keep from laughing. "Why?"

"So I can box your jaw."

She laughed, leaning back against the couch, feeling totally relaxed and very happy. "I love this place," she said, glancing around the dim room, watching the firelight dance on the walls. "Have you had it long?"

"Only a couple of years. I was on the verge of buying a place on the Mediterranean, but I wasn't sure I would get there often enough to warrant the purchase. When a friend told me about this place, I knew it was just what I was looking for. Although I have never been fond of manufactured cities, it's right here in Texas, which makes it convenient.

It's close to Corpus Christi and Padre Island, but isolated enough to give me privacy."

"You should have asked me," she said, her eyes sparkling. "I've always known you couldn't do better than Texas, but what on earth possessed them to name it San Padre? Doesn't that mean saint father?"

He shrugged. "Don't ask me. But since they originally intended to call it Laguna Madre del Puerco—which I think has something to do with a pig, I count myself lucky." He paused, visibly enjoying her laughter as he leaned back beside her. Sliding a casual arm around her shoulders, he said, "I take it you're fond of the Lone Star State."

"I love it. Sometimes I get the feeling that when people talk about the ugly American, they're picturing someone with a Texas accent and a cowboy hat. But that's only because Texans have strong personalities." She chuckled. "And I have to admit that sometimes we can be overpowering for the uninitiated. Texans don't believe the old adage, Less is more. They think even more is not enough. Which makes us perfect for imitation—by the way, I forgot to warn you I like making speeches," she said in a wry aside. "Texans are the most easily recognized people in America in speech and dress. In any town in Texas you'll find the warmest, friendliest, most open people in the world. Wild and wacky and wonderful. Where else would you find a state legislature that stayed up all night debating whether or not to round pi off to three?"

He laughed softly. "They didn't," he said.

"Oh, yes, they did," Glory said, leaning against him, enjoying the feel of his chest beneath her.

Slowly the humor faded from his expression. They gazed at each other in silence, a strange intensity growing between them. She felt as though she had just touched a hot wire. The most incredible sensuality swelled between them, and without volition she leaned toward him, aching to feel his lips against hers.

This is it, she thought. This is finally the right time. She wasn't even worried about admitting to herself that she was more than ready.

But when he moved, it was only to brush a gentle kiss across her forehead. "Bedtime for you," he said softly.

Her eyes widened, the pupils dilated in surprise. "Bedtime?"

He stood, pulling her to her feet. "We can talk more tomorrow," he said as though he were cajoling a four-year-old. "Right now you need your rest."

He was treating her like an invalid aunt, she fumed as she walked to her solitary bedroom.

Eleven

"Do I look like a giraffe?" Glory yelled as she leaped wildly for the Frisbee. Catching the green disk on the tips of her fingers, she returned it immediately while Alan stood laughing. "Laugh now," she said triumphantly as it sailed toward him.

He had to lunge out into the surf to catch it, splashing through the water with awkward movements, but catch it he did. He pointedly ignored her rude comment, and, instead of throwing the Frisbee back, he walked to her side and pulled her down on the sand.

"Rest time," he said, studying her flushed face.

"What are you, my nanny?" she asked dryly.

In the preceding two days a pattern of sorts had evolved. Both being exceptionally fond of the spoken word, they had spent a good deal of their idyll participating in what amounted to debates on any wild subject that came to mind. Other than that,

Alan very firmly made certain that she ate and rested and got plenty of sun.

And not one solitary finger had he laid on her in that time, Glory thought in chagrin. It was making her crazy.

Wiping his face with a white towel, he leered comically. "I want you in tiptop shape when I pounce on you."

"Sounds pretty weird to me," she said, letting her fingers enjoy the texture of the sand. "Do you put all your women in training?"

One thick dark brow rose in inquiry. "Are you one of my women?"

Glory wrapped her arms around her knees. "Well, not yet," she said, somewhat amazed by this astounding conversation. "But that is the general idea, isn't it?"

His gaze swept over her body. "Most definitely," he said, his voice equally casual. "I call it the dreaded-revenge scenario. The one where Randy Villain—boo, hiss—comes to collect on a dubious debt from our delicate but dedicated heroine, Miss Glory—oh, no, gasp, shudder. Twisting his handlebar mustache, our villain demands payment while his eyes are fixed on forbidden"—his gaze dropped to her breasts—"but oh-so-tempting territory."

As she listened to his silly tale, Glory had picked up a handful of sand. Now, raising it above his head, she released it slowly, watching it make a small pile on the top of his dark disheveled hair.

Alan didn't blink an eye, but merely sat in silence for a moment. Then he said quietly, "Glory?"

"Yes, Alan?" Her lip quivered.

"Did you just pour sand on my head?"

Stealthily she began to scoot out of reach. "Sand? On your head?" she asked in confusion. "Whatever can you mean?" Then she snapped her fingers as though a thought had just occurred to her. "Oh, I know. It was probably a sand devil. You've heard of them, of course."

He shook his head slowly, causing grains of sand to trickle down his face. "No, no, I can't say that I have."

"Well, they're sneaky little rascals, I can tell you." She tutted in censure. "Kind of like the sandman, only they don't get you when you go to sleep. They get you when you're trying to seduce innocent maidens." She glanced at him in wide-eyed innocence. "You run across them a lot in Victorian novels and . . . and in Byronic poetry. Your little vignette probably confused them."

He nodded in understanding, but his hand, lying casually on the sand, clinched around a fistful of sand. "Byronic poetry, you say?"

Glory wasn't foolhardy; neither was she slow. Within seconds she was on her feet and running down the beach away from him and the vengeful gleam in his eye. But if Glory was quick, Alan was quicker. She hadn't made ten yards before he tackled her with irritating deftness. They fell together to the sand, rolling and laughing.

From above her Alan watched her lovely laughing face in fascination. And his mind recorded the exact second the laughter faded from her eyes to be replaced by wariness, and beneath that, a glittering sapphire desire that made him catch his breath. The next few seconds seemed to take place in slow motion as he watched her reach up to him. Her slender fingers played with the fabric at the open neckline of his shirt, and slowly she pulled him toward her.

His lips covered hers in a hungry movement. He felt the expected explosion of desire, the visceral warmth invade his system, and he couldn't stop. He wanted her now, right now, right here on the sand.

His hand was shaking when he reached inside her blouse to cup one small, perfectly formed breast. Moving his body against hers, he felt her pelvic bone press against his lower abdomen. He had not known until this moment that a pelvic bone could be so exciting, so sensual.

Their bodies strained together, their movements becoming more urgent. Now, he thought feverishly, it's got to be now. If he couldn't feel the length of her naked body against his soon, he would go crazy.

But she thinks it's revenge, a voice from inside reminded him. And although he tried desperately to ignore the warning, Alan found he couldn't.

Tensing every muscle, he rolled abruptly away from her. He lay facedown, spread-eagle on the sand, his breathing heavy and harsh.

For an endless moment Glory felt as though her skin had been peeled away, exposing raw, vulnerable nerves. She lay there staring with dazed eyes at the sky above, trying to force the world back into perspective.

It seemed like hours later when she came to her knees and bent over him where he still lay on the sand.

"What are you doing?" she whispered, afraid of interrupting some kind of weird meditation rite.

"The multiplication table." The words were muffled and so wry, she had to stifle a giggle.

Moving abruptly, he stood, reaching down to pull her to her feet. "Go have a nap," he said calmly, as though nothing had happened between them, as though they hadn't almost made love under the blue canopy of sky. "We're going out to dinner tonight."

Glory's head swam at this sudden change in Alan. "Dinner?" she echoed, the meaning of the word seeming to temporarily escape her.

With a hand to her back he pushed her in the direction of the house. "Go on, rest."

Fifteen minutes later, while Glory lay on her bed, her eyes were wide open, staring blankly at the ceiling. She had never been able to sleep during the day. And now it was even more difficult than usual.

She let her mind play over everything that had happened in the three days she had been there. She was positive Alan desired her and had from the beginning. It was the reason she was with him.

So why hadn't they made love? she wondered in exasperation. She hadn't exactly been unreceptive.

Unreceptive? she thought, giving an unladylike snort. She had been downright forward. What was with the man?

It was those blasted hormones again, she decided, rolling over to punch her pillow in frustration. They wouldn't leave her alone. For years Glory had buried herself in her work, ignoring any weak, random urge she might have had to utilize her femininity. Then suddenly a man appeared in her life who provoked not random but very pointed, massive urges that couldn't be ignored.

How could Glory have known she was sitting on a time bomb? She supposed she was lucky she hadn't run into a man like Alan during medical school, when this kind of mind-swamping attraction would have buried her career.

But then, she thought, biting her lip, was there another man like Alan: Did another man exist who could pull at her senses the way this one did?

Hastily she shook the thought away. She was being ridiculous. Booger was right. What she felt was simply a matter of chemistry. There wasn't any deep, intricate reason for the attraction. It was as basic as birds mating in the spring. Her nunlike lifestyle of the last few years simply made it feel more urgent. As soon as they made love, her life would return to normal and things would appear in the proper perspective.

But when? she asked herself again, this time sensations of desperation washing through her.

An hour later, without ever having closed her eyes, without ever having found adequate reasons for Alan's behavior, Glory left the bed to dress for dinner.

In the shower decorated with tiles of big poppies, she ran soapy hands over her body with automatic strokes, a frown worrying her forehead. The questions were driving her crazy. Why? When? And what was going on?

Then her movements stopped, her frowning countenance changing to one of enlightenment. She had it, by George, she thought in amazement. She finally knew what was going on and almost laughed in relief.

Alan had brought her here to even the score. That much she knew for sure. But this revenge was not to *make love* to her; his revenge was to *not* make love to her. He was going to tease and titillate until Glory was going crazy for him.

And it was working like a charm, she admitted, giving her head a rueful shake as she stepped from the shower.

Slowly her lips curved in a smile of genuine admiration. It was a plan worthy of him. Pure genius. She had rejected his advances several times. Now that the tables were turned and he was the man in control, he wanted her to experience the same frustration. He wanted her as helpless as he had been when her roommates taped him up. And Glory had played along like a tethered lamb.

But no more, she decided as she rubbed her body vigorously with a towel. Two could play his little game. Alan hadn't been faking when he kissed her on the beach. He wanted her as badly as she wanted him. It was only his pride that was stopping him. She would just have to make sure the waiting was a hardship for him too.

Walking back into the bedroom, she moved to the closet and pulled out the dress she had decided was exactly right for tonight. She gazed at it for a reflective moment, then nodded in satisfaction. Returning to the bathroom, she began to arrange her dark hair.

Alan stood at the glass doors, staring out as though thoroughly mesmerized. The moon was bright, lighting the gulf and the beach. It was a beautiful night and couldn't be responsible for the frown twisting his strong lips. He hadn't, in fact, even noticed the beauty of the silver-brushed sea-scape. His mind was on Glory, as it had been almost constantly since the first night they had met.

He had intended to get her away from her work and her friends so she could rest. Her fragility worried him more than he wanted to admit, even now. And he had wanted to get her away so they could get to know each other. He had hoped that if they were together twenty-four hours a day, she would come to trust him, to like him.

Okay, he admitted silently. He had hoped for more. He had hoped they would become lovers.

But he hadn't reckoned on her extraordinary reasoning. She was willing, even determined, to pay him back for the humiliation she felt he had suffered. But Alan didn't want to be paid back. He wanted—

The thought was interrupted as he heard her enter the room. Forcing a smile, he turned, then stopped jerkily, the smile fading.

It was a recreation of the night they met; the

same heart-stopping emotion filled his chest. The same incredible beauty filled his senses.

She wore the same dress, off-the-shoulder and sapphire blue to match her eyes. Her black hair was caught at the nape of her neck in a roll. And she looked even more lovely than the first time.

Alan moved closer, drawn to her as if by an invisible force. When he stood directly before her, he was still for a moment, taking in her stunning beauty. The satin smoothness of her skin beckoned, and without volition his hand reached out to touch her neck.

Glory found she couldn't look away from the intense fire blazing in his dark eyes. His warm hand on her neck, so seemingly innocent, was the most blatantly erotic caress she had ever experienced.

"This is what I wanted to do that first night," he said roughly. He ran his fingers down her neck to her shoulders, then laughed, a sound so husky it sent shivers up her spine. "I ought to murder you for that charade. You're much too good an actress."

A smile trembled on her lips. "You should have seen your face," she murmured. "You were trying so desperately to be polite."

His hand slid to her neck, spanning her slender throat, the fingers resting on one side, the thumb on the other. "You enjoyed every minute of it," he accused her, his eyes laughing. "I should strangle you right now before you can do any more damage."

Her eyes never left his, but the lids drooped

slightly, effectively telling him she knew strangling wasn't what he had in mind at all.

Drawing in a sharp breath, he moved closer. Glory tensed in expectation, then he seemed to catch himself.

"Dinner," he said shortly, his voice sounding hoarse. "And no more tricks."

"Tricks?" she asked, smiling.

"Oh, yes," he muttered as they walked together toward the door. "You very definitely need strangling."

The restaurant he took her to was small but elegant, specializing in seafood. Floor-to-ceiling windows overlooked the gulf. A combo played mellow jazz and bluesy numbers as Alan and Glory ordered their food.

Handing the menu back to the waiter, Glory looked around the dining room. Delilah would love this place, she thought suddenly. The blonde had a penchant for elegance. Thinking of Delilah brought the roommates to mind, and Glory wondered what they were doing. Suddenly she realized that the apartment, her friends, and her work seemed very far away. She hadn't thought of medicine all day.

"You're frowning," he said, laying his hand over hers. "No frowns allowed tonight."

She glanced up, meeting his eyes to smile, but the smile was troubled. "No frowns," she promised.

"You're thinking about your work, aren't you?" he asked quietly.

"Does it show?" Her smile was honest now. "Did you see a caduceus in my eyes?"

"No," he said, his lips twisting wryly. "Just a little guilt. As though you should be stitching someone up instead of having a night on the town."

She shrugged, acknowledging the truth of his observation. "It's such a part of me; I can never get completely away from medicine."

"You love it." The words were a statement rather than a question.

She nodded. "I love it. As frustrating and hopeless and maddening as it is sometimes, I love it. You go into med school with such high ideals, all fired up with the idea of healing the world." She laughed breathlessly. "Then reality sets in and you're petrified. You're expected to learn hundreds of pages of material a day; what if you forget it all? What if your mind goes blank at a crucial moment?"

She leaned back in her chair, her eyes focused on the past. "You just hope and pray that when you finish your training, you'll know all those things, and amazingly you do. Because if you don't, you're out. But the kicker is that so do the incompetents, the ones you figured would be culled out in med school. Any idiot, given long enough, can memorize facts. Sooner or later they learn the procedures, the rules. Then you realize that med school was a snap compared to what's coming up. Suppose you're one of the ones who shouldn't have made it through. What if you miss something vital? What if a better doctor could have saved this life?"

She raised her gaze to stare at him, wide-eyed. "We're dealing with *life*, Alan. I can't think of that very often because it scares the hell out of me. It's easy to let that fact slide away. Somehow in the process of examination and testing and probing, the patient becomes a list of symptoms. Some doctors accept that automatically, but somewhere inside I've fought against the idea from the very beginning." She shook her head. "Maybe that makes me inadequate in some way. I'll go along doing my job, then all of a sudden it will occur to me that these are *people*, people who think nothing of turning their lives over to me or someone like me.

"The total trust is frightening," she said huskily. "A couple of weeks ago in radiology a man needed a barium enema. The nurse called for Mr. Jones in the waiting room. The enema had already been given before they found out it was the wrong Mr. Jones. The man was there with a friend, but because someone in the medical profession told him he needed it, he allowed it without a word." She raised a hand, palm up, a helpless gesture. "They trust us completely, and in return we treat them like cars in a repair shop."

After a moment Glory blinked, then glanced at the waiter who had arrived with their food, and laughed softly in embarrassment. "I told you I was fond of giving speeches. You have just heard lecture number ninety-three . . . and I apologize most sincerely for the soapbox."

He ignored her comment as he studied her face. "Are you a good doctor?"

The question startled her. "Yes," she said, then more firmly, "Yes, I am. Why do you ask?"

"I already knew you were; I just wanted you to remember it. Your patients will never have to worry about incompetence or callousness." He picked up her hand, running his thumb over the palm. His lips twisted in a smile as he held her eyes. "Even a conscience," he said softly. "An overabundance of virtue. Beauty, wit, intelligence, compassion, and now conscience. You're perfect."

Her laugh was breathless as she felt vibrant warmth flood her body. "Right now I feel perfect," she confessed, then inhaled deeply in an excess of exhilaration. "I feel perfectly perfect."

He laughed, his dark eyes sparkling. "Have you always wanted to be a doctor?"

"Maybe, somewhere in the back of my mind. But the idea didn't exactly solidify into a life plan until my uncle Paul came home with tales of medical school."

"Your uncle was a doctor?"

She stared down at her hands. "He was in his third year of med school when he died. That's a big part of my problem with Daddy. When Uncle Paul decided to study medicine, Daddy tried to talk him out of it. It's not that he had anything against doctors then, he simply didn't think Paul was strong enough to get through the rigorous training. Paul insisted and was accepted to the same school in Dallas that I went to. But as it turned out, Daddy was right."

"What happened?"

She drew in a slow breath. "It was in the begin-

ning of that third year when I started noticing he
was different, more moody, thinner. I found out
later that he was barely managing to keep up with
his studies. The pressure must have been driving
him crazy. He started running with a wild crowd
and . . . well, you can probably guess the next
part."

"Drugs?"

She nodded jerkily. "He died by himself in his
apartment. An overdose."

"God, I'm sorry, Glory."

The real caring in his voice brought quick tears
to her eyes. "It just didn't seem real for me. But it
was worse for Daddy. I never saw him grieve
openly, but he has never forgiven the medical profession or Dallas . . . or himself for Paul's death.
That's why it's so difficult to think of telling him
that I'm a doctor. In the beginning I thought all I
had to do was prove that I could make it through
med school, and Daddy wouldn't be scared for me.
But each day it gets harder and harder, always
knowing in the back of my mind that I'll forever
remind him of Paul's death."

"That's a tough one all right," he said with real
feeling. After a moment he sought her eyes. "It's
going to be painful, but you know you're going to
have to do it someday, Glory. The longer you put it
off, the harder it will be."

She frowned. "You make it sound very simple.
Just go tell him and get it over with. What you
don't seem to understand is that I could be
handing him automatic pain for the rest of his
life." She sighed heavily. "Alan, I hate the thought

of hurting him, but you see"—she raised her eyes to his—"I can't *not* be a doctor. It's not what I do. It's what I am."

"Don't sound so apologetic," he said. "I understand perfectly. I feel the same about my work."

"You do?"

He laughed. "You sound skeptical. Business must sound dry and lifeless to you. But to me it's the most exciting and challenging job in the world." His smile was wry. "I'm very good at what I do."

"I didn't doubt that for a minute," she assured him earnestly. "I imagine you would be good at whatever you choose to do."

"Being the firstborn, you mean?" he asked, his eyes sparkling with humor.

"Being Alan Spencer, I mean."

He glanced over his shoulder at the combo. "Are you ready to test that theory on the dance floor?"

Glory went into his arms willingly. Not only was she aching to have his arms around her, but it was time to get on with her plan. It was time to put an end to the foolishness. She wanted Alan and he wanted her. It was that simple. And tonight was the night.

On the small dance floor she moved as close to him as she could without standing behind him. She felt him stiffen for a moment, then he relaxed, as though realizing they were in a safe place.

Safe? she thought, her lips curving in a provocative smile. She would show him how safe it was. She moved against him in rhythm with the sultry music.

"Glory," he said, his voice husky in her ear, "what exactly do you think you're doing?"

"Can't you tell?" Leaning away from him slightly, she glanced up at him in inquiry. "I must be losing my touch . . . I'm dancing. Of course, I'm a little out of practice, so I guess it's understandable that you can't tell."

She laughed softly when he jerked her close again, muttering, "You devil," against her brow.

When the music ended, he took her hand and pulled her off the dance floor. "I think it's time we went home," he murmured.

"My thought exactly," she said congenially.

Glancing at her briefly, he muttered, "You're looking for a beating, my girl."

She raised one slender brow. "There you go, getting kinky again. And I left all my leather in Dallas."

He stared at the ceiling for a moment, then pulled her in the direction of the door.

On the way home he was silent, but the waves of sensuality between them filled the car. His breathing had still not returned to normal, and Glory herself felt a strange constriction in her chest. She wanted to slide over and sit next to him, but if he felt anything like she did, he was already distracted enough.

Somewhere on the way home, in the intimacy of the closed car, it stopped being a plan, a game. She ached all over, as though she had contracted a strange virus. The need for him went clear to the center of her being.

Alan had not spoken a word when they arrived at

the beach house. Following him into the house, Glory felt almost panicky at the thought of saying good night. She had a terrible feeling that tonight was going to be like all the other nights, and she didn't think she could stand it.

In the darkened living room she watched as he stooped to build a fire in the fireplace. Without turning around, he said, "You need your rest. You'd better get to bed now."

Slowly she walked toward him. The clenching of his fists told her he knew she was there, but he didn't speak, as though his silence would drive her away, as though he thought she would give up so easily.

When she stood directly behind him, he rose and swung around to face her. "Dammit, Glory, can't you take a hint? I'd like to be alone. Go to bed."

Staring up at him, she smiled wistfully. He moaned, reaching out to pull her into his arms. Burying his face in her neck, he said, "You stubborn witch. Is this what you want?" He slid the fabric of her dress down until he exposed the top of one breast. His lips burned a trail to the soft mound.

"Yes," she gasped. "Yes, this is what I want."

They sank together to the fur rug before the fireplace. Their fingers began to act of their own accord—unzipping, unbuttoning—until the upper flesh of each was bare to the eager hands of the other.

Glory pressed her breasts urgently against his hard chest, reveling in the sensuous, scratchy feel of him. He reached up to cup one breast, and she glanced down, mesmerized by the sight of his fingers spread out over the throbbing flesh, one long finger moving across the hardened tip. She watched as he moved down to capture the peak in his mouth, and gasped in pleasure when she felt the sucking pressure.

Her hands restlessly moved across the breadth of his shoulders, the strength of his back. She wanted to touch all of him. She wanted to explore every part of him until she knew him by heart.

When he raised his head, bringing his lips to hers, the heat between them was incredible, searing the sensitive flesh. Their lips were opened wide, as though each was attempting to devour the other.

He cupped her buttocks, pulling her closer, urging her into his hard strength. When his lips sought the tender, sensitive flesh below her ear, she said in a breathless whisper, "This is it." Glory was barely aware that she spoke, and she addressed no one. "This must be what they mean when they say revenge is sweet. So sweet," she said hoarsely, moving into the caress.

She moaned, her hand clasping his neck to hold his lips close. She felt she would never get enough of the feel of him. She wanted it to last forever.

Then something happened. Alan pulled away, and for a moment stared down at her, his eyes looking as dazed as she felt. Slowly, painfully, he left her.

He rose from the floor, moved across the room, and opened the door of a small wooden cabinet. He hauled out a bottle of bourbon, poured half a glass full, and downed it in one swallow.

"Alan," she said hoarsely, pulling her dress over her breasts as a devastating chill hit her. "Alan, what is it? What's wrong?" She rose shakily to her feet.

When he turned back to her, his face was calm, but the scar on his cheek twitched slightly. "Go to bed, Glory."

His voice and eyes were completely devoid of emotion. He would have spoken to a stranger on the street in precisely the same tone of voice.

Glory stared in bewilderment. She couldn't make her mind work. It was still foggy with desire. She took a step toward him, then when she saw him flinch, she stopped. After staring at him for a long moment, she turned and slowly walked out of the room.

Twelve

In the darkened bedroom Glory lay on the bed, the covers pushed aside. The heat made her restless. But it was not the temperature of the room that bothered her, it was internal heat, the heat of her body and mind.

How could she possibly sleep with the scene in the living room playing over and over again in her thoughts? She kept seeing Alan's hard body bathed in firelight, his hands dark on her pale breasts.

A sound that was almost but not quite a moan escaped her, driving her from the bed. She paced back and forth restlessly. If only he weren't so damn special, she thought feverishly. A man to treasure.

A man to treasure. Suddenly Glory drew in a sharp breath. Sweet heaven, she thought in shock, she had actually fallen in love with him. Why hadn't she seen it before?

Sinking to sit on the bed, she held one hand to her mouth, her eyes stunned. *Wait a minute,* she told herself frantically. *Slow down. Think about this.*

But there was nothing to think about. He had wanted a bit of fun, payment for a debt owed him. And she, like a simple-minded fool, had gone overboard and given more interest on the debt than he ever expected or even wanted. Without realizing what was happening, she had fallen totally, completely in love with him.

It was funny, she thought, so damn funny. But Glory had never felt less like laughing. He had brought her here as an elaborate practical joke, and without effort, without even trying, he had captured her heart.

Glory found it very difficult to breathe. She walked to the window, seeking relief, her eyes fixed unseeingly on the full moon. Glory had never felt this wild drive, and therefore had no defenses against it.

Leaning against the window, she pressed her face to the cool glass, feeling betrayed by her own body, by her own heart. Years of self-control counted for nothing now. It all disappeared at the mere thought of Alan.

Her feverish gaze swept the beach and she stiffened. Alan stood at the water's edge, his hands shoved into the pockets of a black vinyl jacket. For an endless moment he stood like a statue, staring down at the sand. Then he lifted his head and the moonlight caught his features. Even from a distance she could see the harsh lines of his face. He looked incredibly lonely.

Then the panicky fluttering in her heart disappeared. She would face the pain and the panic later, when their time together was over. In the meantime she would make as many memories as she could.

Without giving herself time to think, Glory left the bedroom.

Alan shoved his hands deeper into the pockets of his jacket, feeling more tired than he had in a long time. But he knew he wouldn't sleep. With Glory a few steps away sleep was impossible, especially tonight.

The situation, if viewed from a distance, seemed almost funny. After all these years he had finally found the woman who made his life complete, and she refused to see the love in his eyes. But Alan couldn't look at things from a distance, not when every nerve was painfully alive, every muscle achingly aware of his need for her.

Stretching his back wearily, he told himself that eventually he would get through to her. Glory was very bright. Sooner or later she would catch on. But eventually seemed so far away when he was on fire for her tonight.

Closing his eyes, he leaned his head back. He couldn't allow hismelf to dwell on the scene that had taken place in the living room earlier. If he focused on the way she looked, the way she felt and tasted, he would go out of his mind. He knew without a doubt if he went back to the house now, no matter what he had decided was right, his footsteps would lead him to her bedroom.

You're being a fool, a voice deep inside him said. She was so very willing. *Why not take what you can get and hope for the best later?*

He inhaled deeply. It would be only too easy to give in to thoughts like that. The strength he had once taken for granted had diminished pitifully. But there was enough left to keep him on the beach. When they would make love, when he finally would touch heaven, he wanted her aware of what was happening. He wanted no excuses of revenge and debts between them. When she could admit that she wanted to make love for her sake, not for his, then their future would begin.

In the meantime every minute would seem like a year to his aching, burning body.

Glory walked across the beach toward Alan, her footsteps slow but unfaltering. The sudden alertness in his stance told her the instant he sensed her presence.

When she reached his side, Alan moved his head slightly to study her face, his gaze sliding over the full nylon nightgown that the wind flattened against her body.

She heard only the gentle lapping of the waves as she examined the tense lines of his face, highlighted by moonlight reflected off the water.

After a moment he turned back to stare at the

water. "You should have put on a robe," he said, his voice curt. "You'll freeze to death."

"I'm not cold." She sounded hoarse. Swallowing roughly, she said, "What game are we playing now, Alan?"

Incredibly he laughed, but it wasn't a happy sound. "Is that what you think it is?"

"I don't know," she whispered, wrapping her arms tightly around her waist. "I wish to sweet heaven I did."

Inhaling slowly, he turned to face her. "What is it you want, Glory?"

Is that it? she wondered, frowning. Did he want an admission that she wanted him desperately? Would the score be even then? If that was what he was waiting for, it was certainly no hardship, Glory thought wryly. She had no pride where Alan was concerned.

Meeting his eyes, she said without a tremor, "I want you to make love to me. I want it very much. I feel anxious—no, not anxious. I feel angst; it's an old-fashioned word, but this is an old-fashioned feeling. I don't care why this thing between us has happened; I only know it has. And I can't sleep for wanting you. If we don't make love soon, I'll—"

A rough sound issued from deep in his throat, interrupting her. With urgent movements he scooped her up and turned toward the house. She could feel his heart pounding in his chest as he carried her across the sand.

He crossed the deck but didn't go into the living room. Instead, he entered the house through a sliding glass door that led directly to his bedroom.

Stopping beside the wide bed, he let her slide to her feet, then, reaching down, he grasped the hem of her nightgown and pulled it over her head. Pressing her onto the bed, he knelt beside her, staring at her in silence. After a moment he reached out to run his hand gently down her body, a path of fire, watching as her eyelids drifted down in acknowledgment of the wave of electric warmth washing over her.

"Every time I touch you, I can see an explosion in your eyes," he whispered hoarsely as he withdrew his hand. "A brilliant sapphire explosion. That night I watched you undress, I damn near died from wanting to touch you. I never thought I had voyeuristic tendencies, but the sight of you banished any scruples I thought I had. When I saw you touch your breasts, I thought I would go crazy. I wanted to be the one touching them. Every time you touched a part of your body, I felt the heat on mine."

Alan watched a myriad of expressions play across her face as she listened to his confession. He was mesmerized by the sight of her pale body, as he had been that night. The tips of her breasts were colored dark rose, inviting his touch, his mouth. With the tip of his index finger he rubbed one nipple, reveling in its response. Everything felt new with Glory. It was as though he had never touched a woman before.

"You've buried all this need for too long," he whispered, his voice as intense as his gaze. "But I'm glad. Because that means it's all there waiting for me."

His shaking hand drifted down her stomach, rising with the velvet mound, delighting in the feel of her soft, curly pubic hair. He moved his hand through it gently, feeling it spring up around his fingers. When he heard her suck in a sharp breath, a shaft of heat went straight to his groin, intensifying his own desire.

Glory felt the touch of his fingers on the aching spot between her thighs and almost moaned aloud. She was on fire for him. Reaching up, she pushed the jacket from his shoulders. Her eyes were open only wide enough to see the look of intense desire that distorted his strong features. He allowed her to undress him, but he never took his eyes from her, as though he were trying to memorize all the separate pieces that went to make up the woman called Glory.

When the last of his clothes dropped to the floor, he laid down beside her, close but not touching, and slowly turned her to face him so that she had to meet his eyes. It was agony for Glory to be so close. She could feel the heat emanating from his flesh; she inhaled his musky scent, but still they didn't touch.

When she felt she was ready to scream, he reached out and, a bit at a time, moved her body close to his. First their chests touched, her breasts nestling into the fine mat of hair. Then their bellies came together. And when she felt his iron-hard shaft pressing hotly against the throbbing mound of her desire, Glory lost control. Digging her fingers into his back, she thrust her hips frantically against him.

As though she had said the magic word, he rolled her over and entered her with one hard stroke. And the treasures of the sensual world unfolded before her, surrounding her, overwhelming her. Glory gave herself up entirely to the sensations that shook her. As though no longer controlled by her mind, her body acted in its own selfish interest, seeking and finding pleasure after erotic pleasure.

At some point she was vaguely aware of the abrupt tensing of his body, but his triumphant cry was merely background music for the explosion that shook her to the core.

It seemed like hours before the pounding of her heart gave way to a normal beat. The perspiration covering them both had begun to evaporate when Alan reached down to pull the cover up over them. And silently, contentedly, Glory fell asleep in his arms.

"So when Joey got there, Jenny was sitting in the living room with her boyfriend, completely unaware that Joey knew she had thrown away his favorite sweatshirt," Alan said, his eyes sparkling with fun as they sat on a smooth outcropping of rock overlooking the water.

"Lord, Glory, I wish you could have seen his face. Nothing could have been more innocent when he asked if she was using his gym socks again."

"Wait a minute," Glory said, her voice stern as she tried not to laugh. "Do you mean your brother asked her right in front of her boyfriend? And you let him?"

"That's not all," he said, laughing outright now. "When she said she hadn't seen his stupid socks and to stop bothering her, he very blandly told her to look in her bra because that's where they were last time."

"Oh, no," Glory said, gasping with laughter.

They fell together back onto the smooth rock, laughing like a couple of giddy teenagers, the laughter of each inciting the silliness of the other.

The day was a very rare, very warm Indian summer day. A day to press in a scrapbook. Everything seemed funny because all their senses were heightened. Above them the sun was brighter; below them the water was bluer.

When their laughter died away, Alan relaxed against the warm rock, his hands folded behind his head. With her chin resting in her hand, Glory studied him closely, allowing her gaze to drift over his sandaled feet and the tight faded jeans molding his thighs. The sleeveless blue T-shirt he wore stretched tightly across his muscular chest, his bare arms brown and strong, thick blue veins covered by a sprinkling of dark wiry hair. He looked like a lazy lizard sunning on a rock.

"Glory?" he asked, his voice indistinct, as though he were half asleep.

"Um-huh?" she murmured, intent on her examination.

"There's a fly on my arm. Shoo it away."

She almost laughed. He sounded like a pasha giving orders to his harem favorite.

Peering closely at his arm, she whispered, "Alan, this is a very strange fly. It's—oh, my gosh, it's

Vincent Price." She leaned close to his ear and said in a tiny voice, "Help me! Help me!"

Rolling onto his side, he laughed uninhibitedly, drawing her into his silliness by wrapping his arms around her and rocking back and forth with the laughter. All day they had been riding a natural high that was more potent than any drug.

Several minutes later she inhaled deeply and rolled over on her stomach, staring at the small rocky inlet below. There were pools, some less than a foot wide, in between the rocks, and little sea creatures, captured by the tide, scuttled in and out of the rocks.

"Let's go see," she said, grabbing his arm.

"I'm comfortable, woman," he grumbled. "Why are you pulling at me?"

"I want to see the little water beasties up close."

He pulled her on top of him, his hands cupping her buttocks. "How about seeing the big land beastie up close?"

"Unhand me, sir," she said indignantly. "Science never stops for sex."

He raised one brow. "If that's true, I imagine there must be a dearth of little scientists."

She began to laugh, then, meeting his eyes, felt electricity race through her body and drew in a deep breath. She didn't need the physical change in him to know what he wanted. There was a wonderful, mystical kind of communication between them. They were perfectly attuned.

Lowering her head, she kissed him gently. But gentle was not what he wanted, and for the next few minutes he tried to absorb her.

Glory was starving for him. It felt as though it had been years since she had touched him instead of only minutes. While he unbuttoned her loose cotton shirt, she pushed his T-shirt up his chest and over his head with frantic fingers. Then reaching down, she unzipped his jeans, sliding her hands inside, then around to dig her fingers into his hard buttocks, urging him closer.

She was shaking all over as she helped him remove his jeans then her own. When he entered her, Glory was only vaguely aware of the warm, smooth boulder beneath her and the sound of the waves. All her thoughts were concentrated on the man who was urgently merging them into one.

It was only after the earth shook beneath her and the aftershocks died away at last that Glory looked around them and gasped.

"Alan," she said, slapping at the hand that still cupped her breast. "Alan, we're naked!"

"Um-hmm," he said, his eyes closed. "It's hard to make love through two layers of denim. I can't think that it could even make a very effective birth control device—too porous—but you're the doctor; you'd know more about these things than I do."

Framing his face with rough hands, she forced him to look at her. "Listen to me. We are naked—on the beach."

"Wasn't that a movie?"

Pushing him off, she grabbed her jeans and tried to straighten out the legs which were half inside out. "Good Lord," she said in exasperation. "Did you have to tie them in granny knots?"

He sat up, grinning as he reached for his own clothes. "As I recall, I was in a hurry."

After a frantic, scrambling search, Glory managed to locate her panties in one leg of her jeans and put them on. "What if that little boy had trespassed again? What would he have thought?"

Leaning down, he nipped at one smooth breast with his teeth. "He would think you have beautiful breasts. But you're right. I don't want any five-year-old pervert staring at my Glory's glory."

As she buttoned her shirt, they began walking back toward the beach house. "I'm seeing a degenerate side of you that's very disturbing," she said, her tone condemning. "Have you no shame at all?"

"None," he said sorrowfully. "And that fact has kept me up more than a few nights, I can tell you."

Although she tried very hard not to, she had to laugh. As though the exhilaration flowing in her veins had somehow been communicated to him, Alan reached out and grabbed her by the waist. Sweeping her off her feet, he whirled her around and around in joyous circles.

Glory shared completely what he was feeling. There was an abundance of everything today.

Later, as she watched him standing in the water, his jeans rolled up around his calves, she felt emotion well up inside her. It was a picture she wanted to engrave in her memory. He was everything she could want and more. So much more, it overwhelmed her. The tenderness of his touch, the simple wonder in his eyes when he looked at her, these were things she had never dreamed of, had never imagined possible.

And the feelings within herself were also unexpected. When she had fantasized a future lover, she had imagined feeling satisfaction and contentment. Never in her wildest dreams had she imagined the sensations, the emotions, that bombarded her every minute she was with him.

She loved him so much that a feeling close to pain shook her. She wanted him again. She needed him again.

Running her fevered gaze down his hard body, she watched as he bent to pick up a shell, then held it up in triumph. Turning, he began to speak, then the words died as he gazed into her eyes. Without a word having been spoken between them, he moved to her, reached out for her hand, and together they walked toward the house.

Alan leaned on his elbow studying her while he made lazy circles on her stomach with one finger.

"It's time for dinner," he said, his voice still husky from loving her. "If I have to look at another red snapper or shrimp or oyster, I'm going to throw up. I need *meat*." He gripped her shoulders. "Do you hear? I need red meat—a steak, a rib, a hamburger."

"You obnoxious carnivore," she said, stretching deliciously. "Stop staring at me with that look in your eyes. I'm anemic."

He jumped up from the bed. "I'm going to go into town to get the biggest, thickest, juiciest sirloin you've ever seen. This will be a steak worthy of a

Guinness record, the crème de la crème of boeuf, a veritable Rolls-Royce of steaks."

"Dear heaven, you're drooling," she said in disgust, rolling out of bed to pick up her clothes. She felt curiously replete. "If you want to poison your body with the additives they put in that stuff, not to mention what the cholesterol will do to you, go right ahead."

"Does that mean I should get enough just for one?"

"Only if you place no value on your life," she said sternly.

He laughed, pulling her close to kiss her neck. "Mmmm," he said, then reluctantly released her. "Save that place for me," he added as he left the room.

Glory moved to the window and stood there until she saw him leave the house and back the classic MG out of the garage. As he drove away, she felt an overwhelming surge of warmth just looking at him.

It was crazy, she thought, smiling as she leaned her head against the window. In just one day she knew more about the real person that was inside Alan than she knew about any of her friends. It was as though somehow their brains and their hearts had fused.

She moved away from the window slowly. He had been gone for a little over a minute and she already missed him like crazy. A vision of what it would be like when she was permanently without him attacked her, leaving her weak.

Glory hurried out of the bedroom to escape the

vision. She couldn't think about that now. She refused to think about it. That was the way to heartache.

By the time Alan returned, Glory had stilled the panic in her heart and was able to throw herself into his festive mood. He treated his enormous steak as though he were offering it to the gods in sacrifice. On a portable grill he charcoaled the sirloin while Glory put together a green salad. When the steak was done, rather than use the glass-topped table, they sat on the deck cross-legged as they ate with relish, a feeling of bacchanalia in the air.

After dinner Alan reached down and pulled her to her feet. Taking her hand, he led her down to the beach. They walked slowly, watching the sun sink below the horizon turn the water pink and orange, enjoying the night sounds and the ease with which silence lay between them.

"Too bad we can't bottle this and take it back to Dallas," Alan said softly, tightening his arm around her waist as he stared at the horizon. "Thank goodness you're a 'moveable feast.' "

Glory caught her breath as she realized what he was saying. He wanted them to continue the relationship in Dallas. Her heart began to pound frantically, and she stiffened in his arms.

"What's wrong?" he said, glancing down at her. When he saw her face, he held her away from him. "Why do you look like that?"

Glory bit her lip. What was wrong with her? This was what she wanted, had been praying for. The thought of saying good-bye to Alan had been ripping her up. So why did she once again feel so panic-stricken?

She shook her head jerkily. Stalling for time, she said, "I don't understand, Alan. This is not—I thought—I mean, the debt is paid, isn't it?"

He stiffened as though she had struck him. Then, as she stared in wary silence, his eyes grew immeasurably sad. "Do you honestly believe that's all there was to it—a little time in the sack? A little slap and tickle in the sand? Do you think I'm some kind of stud with notches on my bedpost." Now there was anger in his voice. "Rack up nine more orgasms for the man—is that it?"

He grasped her chin roughly, forcing her to look at him. "Look at me, Glory. Look in my eyes and tell me that's all there is to it." When she didn't respond, he let his hand fall. "Talk to me," he said tightly. "Don't shut me out. At least care enough to *try* to work it out."

Care enough, she thought weakly. If she cared any more, she would die of loving him. She stared down at the sand, trying to give the panicky feeling words.

"I'm scared," she whispered hoarsely. "I looked at you and I realized that if I had to make a choice between you and medicine, I would chuck my career in a minute." She shivered, barely catching his sharply indrawn breath. "That's too much, Alan. Everything I've fought for all my adult life means nothing beside my feelings for you. That's too much power for one person to have over another."

Glory could feel him staring at her. She knew he

was preparing to argue and spoke quickly. "Don't you see? I can't let that happen."

He didn't speak for a long time, and Glory grew tense with the waiting. At last he moved, walking a couple of steps away. Then he slowly turned to face her. "That first night at your father's house," he said quietly, "instinctively I knew something important had happened. Even then, when I thought you were a beautiful cork, I couldn't get you out of my mind or my dreams. And every time I ran into you, it grew even stronger. By the time your friends took a hand in the matter, I was bound body and soul." He laughed softly, a sad, wistful sound. "Glory bound."

Moving forward, he gently raised her chin. "You're upset because of the power you say I have over you. Can't you see you have the same power over me? If I had to make a choice between you and my career, there would be no hesitation. I'd choose you in a minute. But why would I have to? Why does there have to be a choice when we can have both?"

"You don't understand," she whispered huskily. *"I forgot."* Her eyes were troubled as she stared at him. "I completely forgot medicine today while I was with you, making love, laughing. It's been my life and I forgot."

He stared at her silently for a long moment. "I understand that you're running scared and not thinking straight. It's hit you too fast. I've had time to get used to the idea of turning my life, my happiness over to someone else. But you're still thinking that life has thrown you one bitch of a curve ball.

You would figure it out all by yourself, given time. But I don't have time. Every minute we're apart up here"—he pointed quickly to his head, then to hers—"is a lifetime, a painful lifetime."

Every word he spoke was like a lash across her back. Her fists were clenched to withstand the pain. It would go away, she repeated silently over and over. It would go away.

Inhaling roughly, he straightened his shoulders as though they ached. "Glory, if there were an accident up there"—he gestured inland toward lights that indicated houses—"and people were hurt, what would you do?"

She gazed at him in confusion. "I'd go help."

He nodded as though she had given him the expected answer. "What if I were holding you, kissing you. Would you still go?"

"Of course."

He stared into her eyes. "And when you saw a bleeding body, would you be thinking of the way I sing in the shower, the way I make love? Would you be thinking of me at all?"

A shudder shook her as she let the truth of what he said wash over her. It was as though he had unlocked the vault she had hastily built around her mind and her heart. She felt light-headed with the release.

"You're a doctor, Glory." He smiled. "Don't you remember? It's what you are, not what you do. But you're a doctor who happens to love me." He pulled her closer, his eyes never leaving her face. "Right?"

She nodded, slowly at first, then with growing fervor. "Right. Oh, you're so right." She wrapped her arms around his waist. "And I almost blew it. We can work something out. Of course we can." She was weak with the relief of not having to say good-bye to him. "Right now my hours are the pits, and, of course, with my roommates, we won't be able to use my place. But I can come to your apartment—"

She felt him stiffen and glanced up in inquiry. His face was cold, as cold as she had ever seen it.

"You still don't understand, do you?" he said harshly.

Pushing her away, he turned to stare out into the gulf. After a moment he said, "When are you going to tell your father that you're a doctor?"

She sucked in a sharp breath. "What in hell is with you?" she said, almost shouting. "Why do you keep pushing me to tell my father? It's none of your business."

He laughed, a harsh, painful sound. "None of my business," he said slowly, the words tight. "You said Jack put people into compartments. And you can't even see that you're doing almost the same thing, only worse. You've put the separate parts of your life into compartments. Medicine, the room-mates, your father, and now me, the convenient lover."

Alan felt strangely dead as he stared at her lovely face. She looked angry and confused and didn't seem to realize he was fighting for his life.

"This relationship," he said tightly, the words painful as they emerged from his throat, "if you can call it that, is going nowhere—it's dead—unless you can pull your life together. I don't want to be one of the separate parts of your life. Maybe I'm selfish, but I have to be part of the whole."

She ran her hands through her hair in frustration. "Don't do this, Alan. Can't you see you're ruining it for us?"

"There is no 'us' until you tell your father and start living your life as a whole."

The words sounded so final. Glory felt a helplessness that she had never felt before. Somewhere along the line she had lost control of her own life.

"Is that an ultimatum?" she asked hoarsely.

He turned away slightly, giving her a view of his stiff shoulders. It was a long time before he answered, then the words were barely audible. "Take it anyway you want to."

She stared at his back, her lips trembling, her hand outstretched. Then she clenched her fist and brought her hand back to her side. He had no right, she thought, the blood in her temples throbbing painfully. He had no damn right to do this to her. She was willing to compromise, but that wasn't good enough for him. He couldn't accept her the way she was; he wanted to remodel her life to his standards.

Inhaling deeply, she knew she couldn't allow it. There was a blank wall in her mind when she thought of what he was demanding of her.

Turning slowly, her movements mechanical, she began to walk toward the house. It was time to pack.

Thirteen

Dallas, Texas

Alan drove through the renovated section of Dallas, a frown deeply engraved in his face as he forced himself to stick to the speed limit. The windshield wipers, slapping back and forth furiously, kept time with his thoughts.

The past week had been pure hell. He had gone through every emotion in the book. He had been angry—with himself and with Glory. For a while he had fiercely resented her and the way she had carelessly thrown away their happiness.

But the anger and resentment hadn't lasted long. Before he could even try reason, self-pity had taken over. He had overindulged in alcohol on more than one night.

But this morning, when he got a good look at the circles under his eyes, he had gone past the point of worrying about who was at fault and who should come to whom.

Ordinarily pride was a wonderful thing. But without Glory pride was just a word. He wasn't going to allow this to continue. He would take what he could get. She was perfectly free to sacrifice her own happiness, but not his.

Turning the car into the gravel driveway, he shut off the engine and stared up at the third floor where faint lights could be seen through the morning rain. Please, he asked silently, let her be there.

Dodging puddles, he pulled his collar up against the wind-driven rain and made his way quickly to the front door. He walked purposefully up the two flights of stairs, and seconds after he knocked at the door of Glory's apartment, Delilah swung it open.

Immediately the blonde's features froze, the look she gave him filled with so much venom, Alan took an involuntary step back.

"What do you want?" she said tightly. "You've got a nerve showing up here."

Alan fought to keep his voice quiet but firm. "I want to see Glory."

"She's not here." The blonde moved to close the door, but Alan held it open with one hand.

"Where is she, Delilah?" he asked softly. "I need to find her."

Frustration at her inability to close the door showed in Delilah's face. "Just go away," she hissed.

Alan shook his head. He couldn't go away. These were the only people who would know where Glory had gone. "Let me come in for a second . . . please. Can't we simply talk?"

She glanced over her shoulder and evidently got a sign to let him in, for she allowed the door to swing open.

Alan stepped into the room. All the roommates were there, all except the one he needed so desperately. Jack leaned against the kitchen counter, his stance casual, his eyes alert as he drank beer from a brown bottle. And on the couch Booger sat next to a stone-faced Addie.

Alan's gaze traveled around the room, meeting the eyes of each in turn. "I need to find Glory," he said again, trying to keep the urgency out of his voice. "I simply want to talk to her."

Jack snorted in an expression of disbelief. "Like hell," he said. "Is that what you did down at your fancy beach place . . . talk?"

Addie turned to look at Alan, her eyes cold. "She came back from that 'vacation' looking like warmed-over death," she said harshly. "Can you imagine how we felt when she told us that instead of taking a rest, she had been with you? She wouldn't have gone if you hadn't blackmailed her." Her fists clenched in her lap. "She was obviously trying to protect us."

"You hurt her," Delilah said quietly, her voice totally devoid of emotion. "I don't know why or how you did it, but you hurt her like I've never seen her hurt."

Alan stared at them in silent frustration. He felt as though he had been tried and found guilty by a group of his peers. Lowering himself to the overstuffed chair, he stared at the floor for a moment, then he drew in a deep breath and began to speak slowly.

"Didn't any of you look at her before she left?" He glanced up, catching them all staring at him. "Didn't you notice that she was about to come unglued? My God, she was positively transparent." His fingers tightened on the arm of the chair. "Yes, I wanted to get her alone. And yes, I hoped for a closer relationship. But that was secondary. I wanted her to rest and eat regular meals. She was bent on proving she was some kind of medical superwoman, and if someone hadn't stopped her, she was headed for a physical breakdown." He inhaled shakily. "You know, she told me about each of you, about how much she cares about you." He smiled sadly. "She would kill for any one of you. I listened to her go on and on about her good friends, and, heaven help me, I was jealous of you." His eyes narrowed. "But *I* was the one who cared enough to make her take a break. I was the one who made sure she ate and rested and got out in the sun. Not one of her good friends did it."

Now none of them met his eyes. The silence in the room drew out uncomfortably. Finally Booger said, "He's right. She was getting black circles under her eyes before she left, and I think she had lost weight."

He raised his gaze to meet Alan's eyes. "But she was happy. When she came back from her time with you, she looked tanned and healthy, but she also looked like something had broken inside her."

Alan sagged slightly, feeling defeat wash over

him. He couldn't respond because he had no answers for them.

"I need to talk to her," he said slowly. "Surely talking to her couldn't hurt anything. And it might help everything."

"No," Delilah said harshly. "There is no way we'll tell you where she is. You've done enough damage."

Alan felt his last hope slip through his fingers. The only other place he knew to try was her father's house in Austin. He ran shaking fingers through his wet hair, his features harsh. Glancing up, he found Addie watching him with an odd intensity.

"She's working at the clinic on Beale Street," Addie said quietly.

"Addie!" Delilah said, her tone condemning.

"Dammit, Addie," Jack said, setting down the beer with a thud as he moved away from the counter. "Why did you do that? You don't know why he wants to see her. You have no idea what went on in San Padre. For all we know, he might be a pervert who gets his kicks out of torturing people."

Addie glanced at Jack in exasperation. "Now I know why there's a rumor going around that you have a steel plate in your head. Grow up."

Booger, who had been watching in thoughtful silence, said calmly, "Why, Addie?"

She turned her head to stare at him for a moment, then she said, "Look at his face, Booger . . . Occam's razor."

Booger looked at Alan, examining him closely. "If two theories fit the observed facts, accept the simpler one," he murmured, then glanced at Addie. "He loves her?"

She nodded slowly.

Standing, Alan moved to the couch, feeling the weight of the world lift from his shoulders. When he stood beside the stocky, bespectacled but strangely attractive woman, he bent to kiss her gently.

"Thank you, Addie," he said softly. "We'll name the first one after you."

"No!" she exclaimed, blushing slightly. "My name is Adelaide. Don't do that to a helpless kid."

He laughed then turned to leave. It would be all right, he assured himself as he took the stairs two at a time. He would make it all right.

The rain slowed him, but twenty minutes later Alan pulled up in front of an aged, pink brick building on Beale Street. Half the lettering on the front of the building was gone, but at one time it said Beale Street Clinic. Green paint was peeling off the front door.

Alan walked into the waiting room and glanced around. A small pregnant woman read a magazine that rested on her rounded stomach and an old man leaned his head against the wall, staring at nothing in the present. Otherwise the room was empty.

To one side of the room, behind a glass window, a woman with graying blond hair carefully ignored Alan's presence until he tapped on the glass. She slid the glass aside without ever glancing up from the book she was reading.

"I'd like to see Dr. Wainwright."

"Sorry, she's not here," the receptionist said, still reading.

"But she's supposed to be working here today," Alan said, trying to keep the impatience out of his voice.

"She was, but she's not now."

Reaching out, Alan carefully removed the book from her hands and turned it facedown on the counter. The woman glanced up, annoyance forming wrinkles around her tight red lips. Then as she finally looked at him, she sat up straighter, running a hand over her hair.

"How long ago did she leave?" Alan asked.

"About half an hour ago." Now her voice was polite, eager to please. "She was supposed to work the whole day, but she just up and left."

Damn! he thought. He had missed her by thirty minutes. He could have even passed her on his way to the clinic.

"Was she going home?" he asked, frowning. "Did she say?"

The woman leaned closer, as though she were gossiping with a friend. "She said something, but she's always a little weird. I never can understand her."

"What exactly did she say?"

"She said something about bearding a lion in . . . no, wait. She said she was going to beard a lion of industry in his industrial den, whatever that means."

Alan inhaled slowly, excitement causing his pulse to race. She was going to his office. He was sure of it. That meant she wanted to see him.

Throwing a quick thank-you over his shoulder, Alan left the clinic, impatience to see Glory building with every passing minute. The trip to the Spencer-Houghton building seemed to take years. The traffic, always heavy, seemed to have built up just to slow him down.

His nerves were stretched to their limit by the time he reached his office. Riding the elevator to the twenty-second floor, he entered the outer office of his suite.

"Peggy," he said in relief as he approached his secretary. "Is Glory Wainwright here?"

"Oh, Mr. Spencer," she said, glancing up from her work. "You've had three calls from Mr. Newman in Geneva. He wanted to know—"

"Later, Peggy. Have you seen Glory?"

"Glory?" she asked, frowning as she thumbed through her papers as though she could find Glory there. "I'm sorry, I don't know—"

"Hasn't anyone been in to see me? A small woman, very beautiful, with long black hair?" And sapphire eyes to die for, he added silently, a small smile twisting his lips.

"Oh, yes," Peggy said in relief. His secretary prided herself on always having anything he needed at her fingertips. "She came in about"— she glanced at her watch—"about fifteen minutes ago."

"Where is she? Is she waiting in my office?"

Peggy shook her head. "No, I told her that you weren't coming into the office for a few days." Panic grew in the young woman's eyes. "That's what you told me to tell anyone who wanted to see you. Isn't that what you said, Mr. Spencer? Did I do the wrong thing?"

"No . . . no, don't worry about it, Peggy," he said in defeat. "That's exactly what I said." He turned to sit on the edge of her desk, pushing a hand through his hair. "I don't suppose she said where she was going from here."

"Actually, she did say something," the woman said, her voice brightening.

Alan swung around. "She did? What did she say?"

"When I told her you weren't here and wouldn't be in for a few days, she stood there for a couple of seconds. Then, when she turned away, I think she said, 'His apartment.' Does that help you?"

Alan leaned over and kissed her soundly on the cheek. "You're wonderful, Peggy. Remind me to give you a raise." Turning away, he walked briskly toward the door.

"What about Mr. Newman?"

"Later, Peggy."

The flesh around his lips was white with tension when Alan finally reached his apartment. Everything today seemed designed to slow him down.

He didn't know exactly what he was expecting, but it wasn't a note wedged under the number on his front door. He stared at it for a moment, then pulled the note out, leaning against the door to read it. After a moment his eyes closed as he drew in a deep breath.

"Dammit, Glory," he whispered. "Am I going to spend my whole life chasing you?"

Glancing down, he read the note again. *I need to talk to you*, it said. Then simply, *Glory*.

Now what, he wondered, feeling as though he were in limbo. He almost laughed when he thought of the note. *She* needed to talk to him? If he didn't find her soon, he would explode. Straightening his shoulders, he turned and walked away from his apartment.

This time the two flights of stairs to her apartment seemed interminable. Somehow he knew she wouldn't be there, but he would try it anyway. Sooner or later she had to come home.

Addie let him into the apartment, staring in surprise. "What happened? Did she refuse to talk to you?"

Alan shook his head. "No, she wants to talk to me. She just won't stay still long enough to do it," he said dryly. "I don't suppose you've heard from her?"

She shook her head. "Not a word."

"Can I wait here?"

Addie glanced around the apartment, then back to Alan as though he had just asked if she would mind storing an elephant in her living room. Beyond her, Delilah was sitting on the couch with Jack. Booger was half hidden by the refrigerator door.

"Sure you can wait here," Booger said from the kitchen. "Would you like something to eat?" He raised a cereal bowl.

"No, thank you anyway," Alan said, walking into the room. Stooping, he moved aside what he swore was the same pile of lingerie that had been there two weeks earlier.

Jack and Delilah glanced at Alan in passing curiosity, then turned back to the book they were looking through together.

"Is there anyplace else I could look for Glory?" Alan asked after interminable minutes of waiting had passed. "Where could she be?"

Booger shrugged. "Glory's always got something going." He glanced up when the phone rang, then turned back to Alan. "She never sits still for five minutes at a time."

"Glory! Where are you? What on earth are you doing in Austin?"

Everyone turned toward Addie, who was speaking into the phone. Moving quickly, Alan grabbed the phone away from her.

"Glory," he said tightly. "Don't you dare move. Do you hear me?"

"Alan?" Glory asked, her voice confused.

"Did you hear what I said? For heaven's sake, just stay put. I'll be there in an hour."

He hung up the phone and walked quickly toward the door. As he left the room, he heard Jack say, "The armpit. Now, there's an erogenous zone that has been overlooked for years. I remember—"

Alan laughed as he shut the door. He had better grow to love them, because something told him that these kooks were going to be his new family.

Glory watched her father walk back toward the house, then she turned and moved through the garden. The chrysanthemums lining the walk provided riotous color to the grounds of her father's house, but Glory didn't see them.

Her mind played over the scene of a few minutes before. When she had told her father the truth of what she had been doing in Dallas, there had been the expected look of pain in his expression. And it had hurt Glory just as much as she had imagined all these years. Although neither had spoken his name, she knew Uncle Paul had been in both their minds.

Her father's pain had finally given way to anger and belligerence, then, eventually, acceptance. And finally, after they had talked in endless circles, she had seen a growing respect that had brought tears to her eyes.

It was behind her now. And all she had to think about was Alan. She felt her pulse quicken in anticipation and something very close to fear. He had sounded so abrupt over the phone. What did he want? Why was he flying to Austin to see her?

She bit her lip. Maybe he had gotten her note and was going to tell her to forget everything. It was a distinct possibility. She had acted like a fool in San Padre and deserved a fool's punishment.

But please, she begged silently, not that.

After she had left his beach house the week before, her feelings of indignation and anger had lasted for exactly half the flight home. Then she had felt dead. All her emotions had gone into hibernation to escape the pain. Without Alan she knew an emptiness greater than anything she had ever experienced, greater than anything she had ever imagined.

It was only this morning that Glory had finally pulled up enough courage to go to Alan. She didn't care if she had to grovel; she just wanted his arms around her again. But she had met with a dead end in Dallas. Life wasn't going to make it easy for her this time around.

So Glory had come here, to her father. She had come to make a beginning, and she prayed she had not waited too long.

It couldn't be the end, she thought. Fate couldn't be so hard. It was too easy to look back over her life and pick out the parts for which she might be punished now. Every life contained sins, she thought moodily. Had she really done something so terrible that fate would withhold the thing she wanted most?

Moving forward, she sat on a low stone wall and looked out over the still green back lawn of her father's four-acre estate. There was nothing she could do now except wait. It was all in Alan's hands. Her life, her happiness, were in his hands.

Glory felt an electric tingling sensation on the back of her neck, and before she could even glance around, Alan was there. Without a word he sat beside her on the wall. Glory felt her heart jump in her chest, then it began to pound furiously.

He reached down to pick up a loose pebble from the walkway. "I had to wait an hour for a flight out of Dallas," he said conversationally. "It's hard to believe they're getting thunderstorms there when it's so clear here."

She nodded jerkily. "I don't like to fly when it's raining," she said, wincing inwardly at the hoarseness of her voice. "I like to see what's below me." Glancing at her hands, she smoothed them over her slacks nervously. "Addie said you had been at the apartment for a while."

He nodded, then his lips twisted in a small smile. "Did you know your friend is in love?"

"Addie? With whom? Oh, no," she said, the words almost a moan. "Not Jack. Addie may act tough as an alley cat, but she bruises like old Russian royalty. Jack will break her heart for sure."

"Not Jack," he said, his dark eyes sparkling with fun. "Booger."

"Booger!" she squealed in disbelief, then her expression grew thoughtful and she murmured, "Booger. Of course it's Booger." She laughed softly. "He's exactly right for Addie. Why didn't I see it before?" She glanced at Alan. "How did you find out?"

He smiled, a small wry twisting of strong lips. "Kindred spirits," he said.

Glory sucked in a sharp breath, her heart fluttering as though it would fly out of her chest. She stared down at the hands she was twisting in her lap. "I—I told my father."

There was a long moment of tense silence. Then he said simply, "Why?"

"Because it was the right thing to do. Because—oh, what the hell, I told him because you said I had to," she said, her voice disgruntled. "I did it because I wanted to show you I was trying to pull my life together." When she saw the fire blazing in his dark eyes, she added quickly, "It's not that I'm admitting you were right, you understand. But there may have been something to what you said." She exhaled slowly. "Now, are you satisfied?"

"No," he said, his voice husky. "I haven't been satisfied since the last time we made love." He gently raised her chin. "Does this mean you want— really want—to incorporate all the pieces of your life into a whole?"

She nodded, feeling bubbles of exhilaration rip through her bloodstream.

He moistened his lips in a curiously nervous gesture. "Am I a piece of the whole now, Glory?"

She shook her head slowly and felt a shudder shake him. "No," she whispered, wrapping her arms around his waist. "You're not a piece. You're the whole."

He groaned, burying his face in her neck. For a long time they simply sat there, each absorbing the warm, essential presence of the other.

"I couldn't take it," he whispered into her hair, against her neck. "I couldn't take it without you. Maybe I shouldn't tell you, but I would have crawled, Glory. I would have begged you to take me on any terms you wanted. I didn't expect you to meet me halfway."

"It's not going to be easy," she said, the words muffled against his face. "This changing business. I'm going to need help."

"I'll help," he said, and she realized he was laughing. She understood. She felt like laughing too.

She ran her hands over his back, feeling the

familiar muscles and bones. "Extensive help," she murmured. "Constant help."

Framing her face, he stared into her eyes. "It's that serious, huh?"

She moved her head slightly to kiss the palm of his hand. "It may take the rest of my life to get it right," she confessed softly.

"I've got plenty of time," he said. "For you, I've got forever." He lowered his head to kiss her and, joyously, Glory moved closer to forever.

THE EDITOR'S CORNER

We've received the most glorious comments about **SUNSHINE AND SHADOW** from booksellers and reviewers who got advance reading copies of this wonderful novel by Sharon and Tom Curtis! "Pure magic" is what one bookseller called this powerfully evocative love story, and, indeed, "magic" seemed to be the key word in almost everyone's comments. But, as **SUNSHINE AND SHADOW** is on sale at the very minute you're reading this, I'm sure you'll want to get a copy and decide for yourself what is the most appropriate description. Enchanting? Joyous? Poignant? Tender? Touching? Sensuous and sensual? Utterly captivating? I'd vote for all those . . . along with "pure magic," of course, and a continuing string of glowing adjectives. You simply must not miss this exquisitely beautiful and heart-stoppingly exciting love story of two people from completely different backgrounds. Need I add that it is written as only the Curtises could write it?

TOO MANY HUSBANDS, LOVESWEPT #159, is by a delightful newcomer to the ranks of LOVE-SWEPT authors, Charlotte Hughes. In this charming, slightly wacky romance, beautiful, but hassled heroine Meri Kincaid finds herself with too many husbands, indeed. How, you ask, can Meri be out of jail . . . not even facing a longtime sentence for being in this spot? Well, she's not *really* a wife to the twelve grateful bachelors in her life. In a financial fix after the sudden death of her husband, Meri had turned to homemaking to support herself and her young daughter. Now she has her hands full running the homes—and the lives—of those men, so how can she take on yet another client? Enter
(continued)

Lucky Thirteen! He's Chet Ambrose, one handsome hunk of a sweet man who proposes they swap services. She will provide cleaning and cooking for him; he'll use his carpentry skills to prevent her ramshackle house from falling apart. Whew! Talk about falling . . . there are falling ladders (no black cats, though) and a whole lot of falling in love . . . and you'll find yourself falling under a spell as you read this warmhearted and exciting romance.

BEDSIDE MANNERS, LOVESWEPT #160 features more of Barbara Boswell's totally endearing and wonderfully quirky characters. Here, Dr. Case Flynn, whom you met in Barbara's first ever published romance, **LITTLE CONSEQUENCES,** is the hospital lothario. But that sexy devil more than meets his match in Dr. Sharla Shakarian who is not only luscious to look at but an outstanding pediatrician, and a wonderfully warm and wise woman. Case is definitely *not* the marrying kind—not with the parents he'd had! And Sharla's a family-centered lady, if there ever was one. Add to this basic conflict the dramas of the hospital they work in, their well-meaning families and friends, and most of all the raging hunger between them and you have one heck of a delectable romance from one heck of a talented author!

It will be a very long time before I forget the beauty of Fran Baker's first romance for us, **SEEING STARS,** LOVESWEPT #161. Just as Nick Monroe's laugh steals Dovie Brown's heart, so will it steal yours. And Dovie's sweet, but fierce need for love will make you ache for her, just as you ache because of the tragic consequences of an accident Nick had. When these two humorous, fiery, loving people overcome the obstacles that separate them,

(continued)

you'll find yourself cheering! Set in moutain country, **SEEING STARS** is rich in atmosphere and in the exploration of the differences that are only superficial when two hearts beat as one.

Now, sit back and enjoy some big chuckles and large guffaws with **SECRETS OF AUTUMN,** LOVESWEPT #162 by Joan Elliott Pickart. Autumn Stanton just couldn't resist using Graham Kimble in her research. Trying to prove that men respond to the superficial aspects of women, she masqueraded as dowdy Agatha, bright and capable, but definitely plain as ditchwater. Then she fell for Graham even as he seemed to fall for her. How could she have guessed that such a womanizer had sworn off bubbleheaded beauties and was determined to find a woman whose looks were nothing special? This is just the beginning of one of Joan's most delightful romps . . . spiced with tender emotion and inevitable fireworks!

We hope you'll enjoy all the books we're publishing next month as much as we enjoyed helping to bring them to you.

With every good wish,

Carolyn Nichols

Carolyn Nichols
  Editor
LOVESWEPT
Bantam Books, Inc.
666 Fifth Avenue
New York, NY 10103

His love for her is madness.
Her love for him is sin.

Sunshine
and
Shadow

by Sharon and Tom Curtis

COULD THEIR EXPLOSIVE LOVE BRIDGE THE CHASM BETWEEN TWO IMPOSSIBLY DIFFERENT WORLDS?

He thought there were no surprises left in the world ... but the sudden appearance of young Amish widow Susan Peachey was astonishing—and just the shock cynical Alan Wilde needed. She was a woman from another time, innocent, yet wise in ways he scarcely understood.

Irresistibly, Susan and Alan were drawn together to explore their wildly exotic differences. And soon they would discover something far greater—a rich emotional bond that transcended both of their worlds and linked them heart-to-heart ... until their need for each other became so overwhelming that there was no turning back. But would Susan have to sacrifice all she ⌐rished for the uncertain joy of their forbidden love?

/ for full details on how to win an authentic Amish quilt ⌐aying the traditional 'Sunshine and Shadow' pattern in ⌐es of SUNSHINE AND SHADOW or on displays at partici- ⌐ting stores. No purchase necessary. Void where prohibited ⌐ law. Sweepstakes ends December 15, 1986."

Look for SUNSHINE AND SHADOW in your bookstore or use this coupon for ordering: